It appea _____ her charms.

The desire flickering in his suddenly dark depths told her Santa was having some naughty thoughts of his own. The realization gave her the courage she needed to wrap her arms around his neck. "I've always wanted to kiss a man with a beard."

"That's one Christmas wish that's easy to fulfill." Without warning Seth's mouth closed over hers. His hands splayed against her back and he pulled her as tight as his overstuffed belly would permit.

Waves of desire washed over Lauren and she gave in to the moment, until an excited voice cut through the passionate fog.

"Daddy, Daddy, come quick," Dani called from the doorway. "Santa is kissing Miss Lauren."

Dear Reader,

Every author has books that are special to them. Some of my personal favorites are ones that involve children, especially little girls. This is probably because I have a daughter of my own. Children add their own special flavor to a book because, as we all know, you can never tell what's going to come out of their mouths!

But in a romance, children serve another purpose, as well. How the hero (in this case, Seth) relates to his daughter, Dani, tells us a lot about him. To me, there is nothing more sexy and appealing than a man who is a good father.

In falling in love with Seth and choosing eventually to make her life with him, Lauren is also choosing to make her life with Dani. It was important to me to show she would be not only a good wife to Seth, but a good mother to Dani. When I ended this book, I had no doubts these three were perfectly matched and would have a wonderful future together.

That's why I love writing for Special Edition. These are stories about real people finding their happily-ever-after. Seth and Lauren and Dani found theirs. I hope you find yours, too!

Warmest regards,

Cindy Kirk

MERRY CHRISTMAS, COWBOY!

CINDY KIRK

SPECIAL EDITION®

Published by Silhouette Books

America's Publisher of Contemporary Romance

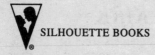

SILHOUETTE BOOKS

Recycling programs
for this product may
not exist in your area.

ISBN-13: 978-0-373-65491-8

MERRY CHRISTMAS, COWBOY!

Visit Silhouette Books at www.eHarlequin.com

Printed in U.S.A.

CINDY KIRK

has loved to read for as long as she can remember. In first grade she received an award for reading one hundred books. Growing up, summers were her favorite time of the year. Nothing beat going to the library, then coming home and curling up in front of the window air conditioner with a good book. Often the novels she read would spur ideas and she'd make up her own story (always with a happy ending). When she'd go to bed at night, instead of counting sheep, she'd make up more stories in her head. Since selling her first story to Harlequin Books in 1999, Cindy has been forced to juggle her love of reading with her passion for creating stories of her own...but she doesn't mind. Writing for Special Edition is a dream come true. She only hopes you have as much fun reading her books as she has writing them!

Cindy invites you to visit her Web site at www.cindykirk.com.

To Patience Smith.
I can't believe it's been ten years since you bought
my first book. Working with you this past decade has
been pure pleasure. I've learned so much from you.
You're knowledgeable, professional but also great fun.
I can't wait to see what the next ten years bring!

To Shana Smith,
editorial assistant, for all your work on this book. I very
much appreciated your insightful comments. You have
a great future ahead of you in the publishing business!

Chapter One

"Are you asking me to move in with you?" Lauren Van Meveren placed the cup on her kitchen counter and stared at the handsome rancher.

Seth Anderssen, known in Sweet River, Montana, for his quick wit, didn't miss a beat. "I guess I am. 'Cept we'll have separate rooms and you'll be there to tend to my daughter's needs, not mine."

Only when he chuckled did Lauren realize how her question actually sounded. She swallowed a groan. For an intelligent woman on the verge of earning her PhD in psychology, sometimes she could be amazingly inept.

"I knew that." She met his gaze and shrugged, the cool response at odds with her rapidly beating heart. "We don't have that kind of relationship. We've never even kissed."

"That could easily be remedied." His eyes took on an impish gleam and she caught a glimpse of the boy who'd once dropped a frog down the front of his sister's dress.

"True." Lauren kept her tone deliberately light. "Pressing lips together isn't that difficult."

"Is that all you think kissing is?"

Lauren thought of the few men she'd kissed. Ones with brilliant minds who appealed to her intellectual side. Ones with a sexual magnetism who appealed to her physical side. "It can be, more or less, depending on the man."

Though she had the feeling with Seth it would be *more*. Since she'd moved to Sweet River five months ago, the way Lauren viewed him had changed dramatically. He was no longer simply the trustworthy older brother of her good friend Anna, the guy she'd met her freshman year in college when he'd driven to Denver to move his sister into the dorm.

At thirty-two, the widower and doting father of one was a well-respected rancher and head of the local cattlemen's association. He was a man who—despite his own obligations—had gone out of his way to help her find subjects for her dissertation research. And with his dark blond hair, scintillating blue eyes and superbuff body, he was, hands down, the hottest guy in Yellowstone County.

However, unlike other single women in Sweet River, Lauren didn't have happily-ever-after designs on him. Seth's roots in this ranching community ran deep. And no matter how much she'd enjoyed her stay, it didn't take an IQ of one hundred and sixty to know she'd never be able to realize her dreams here.

"Forget about kissing for a minute," Seth said. "Will you do it, Lauren?"

Do it? Her eyes widened in surprise before she shook herself and jolted herself back to reality. "Hmm?"

"Will you move in and help me take care of Dani?" His tone was low, persuasive and sexy as hell.

The air between them thickened. Beams of light spilled through the lace curtains, turning Seth's hair to spun gold. The dark blue depths of his eyes beckoned, tempting Lauren to step off the firm shore of complete control to a place where she could be over her head in seconds. His cologne teased her nostrils, the woodsy scent making her feel warm and tingly inside.

Lauren wanted nothing more than to say yes. But she'd never acted impulsively and she wasn't about to start now.

"I understand the predicament you're in, what with your housekeeper being too old to care for an injured child and all." Lauren instinctively slipped into the calm rational tone she used when counseling patients. "However, taking care of a seven-year-old for three weeks is a huge responsibility."

Disappointment skittered across Seth's face and Lauren stifled a groan. Instead of reassuring him, her words had caused him to jump to the wrong conclusion. "I'm not saying that I won't—"

"You don't have to beat around the bush. If you don't want to help us, just say so." He rocked back on his heels and blew out a harsh breath. "I know she can be a handful, even when she's well, but with a broken leg and arm—"

"This isn't about Dani." For a woman who prided herself on her communication skills, she was doing an abysmal job with this conversation.

"I don't understand." Seth's intense blue eyes pinned her. "Is it me? Have I offended you in some way?"

"Not at all."

The lines furrowing his brow eased and a look of relief crossed his face. "Then what's the problem?"

"I want to be certain my work won't interfere with my being able to care for Dani." Not only did Lauren need to finalize her dissertation research, her counseling practice had grown consistently since she'd begun seeing clients several months earlier. She had to figure out how she'd be able to fit those sessions into her schedule and meet Dani's needs, too. "Could I give you my answer in a few days, say right after Christmas?"

Anna had told her Seth had already made arrangements for one of the ranch hands to do his chores until January 1, so he could care for his daughter over the holidays. With Christmas being the day after tomorrow, if she said no, that would give him a week to find someone else. But Lauren hoped she'd be able to help him out. Dani was a precious little girl and Seth was a decent, hardworking man in a tough spot.

"After the holiday will work," Seth said, surprisingly agreeable.

"I'm really not trying to put you off," Lauren said.

"I know you're not. You have valid concerns. My daughter isn't going to be an easy one to watch." Seth's lips quirked upward. "She's going to find those activity limitations hard to bear."

"Keeping her occupied and stimulated *will* be a challenge." Still, Lauren appreciated the child's headstrong nature. In many ways Dani reminded Lauren of herself at that age. Perhaps that's why she felt a special affinity for the little girl. She remembered the shock she'd felt when Anna had called and told her about the accident.

"Dani was incredibly lucky," Lauren continued. "To end up with just a couple broken bones is nothing short of a miracle."

"I don't know what I'd have done if I'd lost her." Seth's voice thickened and his fingers tightened on the brim of the cowboy hat he clutched in one hand. "I should have made sure John Redmond knew I didn't want her on an ATV."

Seth didn't need to elaborate. Everyone in town had heard the story. How Dani was playing at her friend Emily's house. How Emily's brother, Kyle, had decided to give the girls rides on his ATV. How none of the three had been wearing helmets.

Though hitting a rock in a pasture could happen to anyone, it was rumored Kyle had been going too fast. While the boy had been uninjured when the ATV had flipped, Dani had been thrown a full fifty feet. When the volunteer rescue squad had arrived, she'd been unconscious. The paramedics feared she'd injured her spine. Thankfully she'd only sustained a broken arm and leg and a mild concussion.

"Kids play. They get hurt." Lauren's childhood hadn't been that way, but from the stories her friends told, it was amazing some of them had lived to adulthood. "The accident wasn't your fault."

"It *was* my fault." Seth's eyes flashed. "I'm her father. I promised Jan I'd keep our daughter safe."

Lauren tried to hide her surprise. Seth rarely talked about the hometown girl he'd married in college who'd died from cancer three years ago.

"I understand you feel guilty," Lauren said in a soothing tone. "But some things are out of your control."

He lifted his chin in a stubborn tilt. "If I'd made it clear Dani wasn't to ride the three-wheeler, she'd never have gotten hurt."

It was becoming increasingly apparent to Lauren that nothing would be gained from pursuing this topic further. Seth was responding from emotion instead of logic. She heard the guilt in his voice and saw the pain in his eyes. Though she doubted he'd ever admit it, the rugged Montana cowboy looked like a man in desperate need of a hug.

Impulsively Lauren stepped forward and wrapped her arms around him, just as she always did with her friends Anna and Stacie when they needed comforting. Surprisingly, he let her pull him close. "You're a good dad, Seth," she whispered against the smooth fabric of the coat he hadn't bothered to take off. "Don't let anyone tell you differently."

For a brief moment in time, they stood wrapped in each other's arms. Having this handsome cowboy in her arms was very different than hugging a girlfriend. They fit together perfectly, just like in her dreams. As she breathed in the clean, fresh scent of him, she experienced an overwhelming urge to nuzzle his neck. But Lauren kept her lips to herself. Something told her this wasn't a man who'd be satisfied with a brief fling.

Stepping back, Lauren let her hands drop to her sides. "Can I get you a cup of coffee? I just brewed a pot. I've also got sour-cream cake doughnuts Stacie brought by last night. She's trying some new recipes and wanted me to check them out. I also have a couple of blueberry ones and some—"

She stopped midsentence and clamped her mouth shut. She was babbling—an unattractive quality under any circumstances.

"I'm not hungry but coffee sounds good." Seth's smile was easy, but there was awareness in his eyes that hadn't been there before the embrace.

"Cream and sugar?"

"Black works for me."

Lauren grabbed a mug from the cupboard. She was pleased, but perplexed. When Seth first arrived, he'd mentioned that Connie Swenson, his foreman's wife, was watching Dani this afternoon so he could run errands. Lauren had thought he'd be eager to get home. After all, he'd barely left Dani's side since the accident. Yet now he shrugged out of his heavy coat and draped it over one of the kitchen chairs as if he had all day.

Lauren couldn't pull her gaze from him. The colors in his flannel shirt made his eyes look like sapphires. For a second she thought about telling him so. She smiled, imagining his reaction.

"What?" Seth settled into the closest chair and placed his work-hardened hands on the table.

"I like that shirt," Lauren said. "It's a good color for you."

"Thanks." He glanced down as if he'd forgotten what he wore. "Anna gave it to me for my birthday."

"Figures. Your sister has excellent taste." Lauren poured coffee into a mug, placed it before him then took a seat across the table. "I can't believe she and Stacie are both married."

Stacie had wed rancher Josh Collins in October, and Anna had married Mitch Donavan, a boyfriend from her high school days, just last week, only two days before Dani's accident.

"Leaving you to fend for yourself." Seth glanced around the spacious kitchen, which still retained much of its turn-of-the-century charm. "Do you ever get lonely?"

The old Victorian where Lauren resided had originally belonged to Seth and Anna's grandmother. His sister had inherited it when Grandma Borghild had passed on several years earlier. Now Anna lived with Mitch in the log home he'd built at the foothills of the Crazy Mountains, and Lauren had this big house all to herself. Once she moved out, Anna planned to put the home on the market.

"Not really. I've never minded being by myself." Lauren added a lump of sugar to her coffee and slowly stirred. "I'm an only child. When I was growing up my parents were always busy. I'm good at keeping myself occupied."

His blue eyes filled with understanding as his hands wrapped around the warm mug. "Dani is like that, too. She can play by herself for hours. Which is a good and a bad thing."

Lauren raised a brow.

"I worry about her being alone so much," he explained. "That's why I make sure to spend quality time with her every evening. And to invite friends over to play so she can learn to share and have an opportunity to socialize. I'm sure your parents did the same for you."

Lauren wondered what he'd say if she told him she seriously doubted they'd ever given her needs that much thought. She'd been an unplanned late-in-life baby. Both had been determined not to let her arrival impact their careers.

"They did their best." Lauren kept her answer simple. When it came to discussing her parents, the less said the better. She decided to change the subject. "I can't believe Christmas is this weekend."

"I know." Seth took a sip of coffee. "Are you going home for the holidays?"

"My parents like to spend Christmas in Paris." Lauren found herself strangely embarrassed by the admission. "Going to France has become a holiday tradition for them. Since they live on separate coasts it's a good way for them to reconnect."

Seth's brows pulled together. "They don't live together?"

"They do," Lauren said. "About ten percent of the time."

Confusion blanketed Seth's face. "Are they separated?"

"Only by distance. My father teaches at Stanford." Lauren kept her tone light. "My mother is at Cornell."

Seth's eyes widened but he immediately brought his expression under control. "Yet they're married."

"Thirty-five years next month." Lauren added another lump of sugar to her coffee. "They have a modern 'commuter marriage.'"

It wasn't the kind of union most would choose, but it worked for them. She took a sip of coffee and grimaced at the sweetness.

"Hmm." Seth hesitated, obviously subscribing to the tenet if you can't say something nice, don't say anything at all. "It must be hard, having them both far away."

"I'm used to it." After all, even when she was with them, she felt in the way. "What's difficult is being without Stacie and Anna."

Unexpected tears stung the backs of Lauren's lids. Though Christmas was only a few days away, she'd avoided thinking about the new reality as much as possible. It was too easy to get into "pity party" mode and that wasn't fair to anyone. She was happy for both her friends. Happy they'd found someone they loved. Happy they'd found their bliss in Montana…but not happy to be the odd one out.

"I'm surprised neither of them invited you to spend Christmas with them." A look of disappointment skittered across Seth's face. "That sure doesn't sound like Anna. Or Stacie, either."

"They did invite me," Lauren reassured him. "But they're both newlyweds. I'm not going to crash their first holiday with their new husbands."

"I suppose," Seth reluctantly agreed.

"There's no supposing about it," Lauren said firmly. "They shouldn't have to worry about entertaining me."

"You're being an awfully good sport," Seth said.

Lauren couldn't understand the admiration in his tone. "Anyone would feel the same."

"I wouldn't be so sure of that." Seth paused for a moment. "I've got an idea. How 'bout you join Dani and me? The food won't be anything special but it'll be edible. It'd be great to have another adult around on Christmas Eve, and I know my daughter would enjoy having a different face to look at besides mine."

Before she could politely refuse the offer, Seth reached across the table and took her hand. "I'd really like you to spend Christmas Eve at the ranch."

Lauren was sure he'd meant it only as a kind gesture, an innocent show of friendship. But there was nothing innocent about the jolt of desire that shot through her. Her first reaction was to snatch her hand away, but that would make her look like a fool. Besides, she really liked the feel of his warm, strong touch.

She reminded herself that he was merely showing his support. And his offer was probably no more than any person in this small town would make.

"I make a great prime rib," he added in a persuasive tone. "And I promise the brussels sprouts will stay in the freezer."

Just say no. She could hear her father's stern voice in her head. Concentrate on your dissertation. Your career must be your priority.

Still, Lauren's entire being rebelled against the prospect of eating a frozen dinner in front of a computer screen on Christmas Eve. And really, what would be the harm in accepting Seth's offer? It was just dinner. And she had to eat…

"C'mon, Lauren, say yes." His fingers tightened around hers. "Aside from pleasing Dani, it'll be a great way for us to get to know each other better."

Lauren's heart skipped a beat. When he put it that way, how could she refuse?

Chapter Two

"I told Seth that Dani could move in with Mitch and me until the casts come off." Anna Donavan's words were muffled by the scarf shielding her face from the harsh Montana wind.

Lauren hunched her shoulders and shoved her gloved hands into the pockets of her jacket. She resisted the urge to tell Anna to hurry up and open the door. Anna hated the cold as much as Lauren did and the fact that she'd stayed in town and reopened her shop on Christmas Eve was a testament to their friendship. "I bet your brother just wants to keep things as normal as possible for her. That means sleeping in her own bed."

"That makes sense," Anna said grudgingly, heaving an audible sigh when the store key slid into the lock. She turned the handle, pushed open the door and flipped on the lights before stepping aside to let Lauren slip past.

Lauren could feel her blood start to thaw as soon as the door shut behind her, blocking the wind. A blast from a heater duct provided a warm welcome. After a few seconds, Lauren pulled her hands from her pockets and glanced around. Two gifts shouldn't be hard to find. Not in this store.

Sew-fisticated was the name of the eclectic shop Anna owned, along with one of her former high school classmates, Cassie Els. Cassie was a fantastic seamstress and Anna a talented designer. In addition to custom-designed clothing, they offered clothing repair, knitting classes and quilting supplies. And for Christmas the store had been stocked with a variety of popular gift items.

"I didn't know you were starting quilting classes." Lauren stared at the brightly colored notice on the community bulletin board.

"Cassie will be doing the teaching. I'll be doing the learning." Anna pulled the scarf from her head, sending flakes of wet snow flying.

"You?" Lauren didn't bother hiding her surprise. Anna had always been the trendiest and most fashion oriented of the three friends. "Quilting doesn't seem like your thing."

"That's what Mitch said." Anna laughed, her voice filled with love for her husband of ten days. "Actually that's not true. What he said was I'm constantly surprising him."

The way her face glowed, Lauren surmised that Mitch was enjoying the surprises. "But *quilting?*"

"It's very fashionable," Anna said. "Just like knitting. Women are searching for something real, something they can hold in their hands."

Lauren's skepticism must have shown because Anna chuckled. "I know it's a change for me, but the design part of the process fascinates me. Plus I like the idea of making something that can be passed down from one generation to another."

While that was a rather old-fashioned concept, Lauren recognized the appeal. "Makes sense."

"You could join me," Anna urged. "It'd be more fun to learn with a friend."

"Um, no thanks. Not my thing." Lauren moved to a counter showcasing several varieties of men's gloves. She took off her mittens and touched a pair made of soft pig suede. "Do you think Seth would like these?"

Anna moved to Lauren's side and studied the gloves with a critical eye. "These are lined with soft acrylic pile for added warmth. And they're nice enough to wear when he goes out, but sturdy enough for some of the lighter ranch work."

Lauren smiled at her friend's enthusiasm. Anna had worked retail for years before opening her own shop. It was easy to see why she'd been so successful. "I'll take the gloves for Seth and that necklace with the pink heart for Dani."

"I'll wrap them for you." Anna took the gloves from Lauren's hands and removed the necklace from a display. Even as she put the items in stenciled gift bags, she glanced at Lauren. "My brother wouldn't expect you to bring gifts."

"I'm sure you're right." Lauren lifted one shoulder

in an unconcerned shrug. "But he was nice enough to invite me to share his Christmas Eve and I want to bring something."

"You could have come to my house." Anna tied each bag shut with a red raffia bow. "Both Mitch and I wanted you with us."

The sincerity in her friend's tone brought a lump to Lauren's throat. Stacie had assured her of that same fact just this morning. Having two such wonderful friends almost made up for not hearing from her parents.

"You and Stacie are the best," Lauren said. "But you have husbands now—"

"I told you—"

"—and besides, this will give me a chance to get to know Seth and Dani better." Since her conversation with Seth yesterday, Christmas Eve with him and his daughter had been constantly on Lauren's mind. She couldn't believe she hadn't thought of bringing gifts until this afternoon.

"It looks like the snow is picking up." Through the front window of the shop, the streetlight illuminated the swirling flakes. "You're really going all the way out to the ranch for just a few hours?"

"Actually—" Lauren struggled to keep her voice casual and offhand "—I'm spending the night."

Seth wheeled his 4x4 to the curb in front of his sister's shop and parked behind his brother-in-law's Jeep. In the half hour it had taken him to drive from his ranch into Sweet River, the snow had started to pick up, making it increasingly difficult to see.

Pulling his hood up over his stocking cap, Seth

opened the door and stepped into the brisk north wind. He raised a hand in greeting to Mitch and waited for his friend to get out of the Jeep. If you factored in the wind chill, the temperature had to be below zero.

"Cold enough for you?" Mitch slammed the door of his Jeep and jammed his hands into his pockets.

"This?" Seth scoffed. "Practically balmy."

"Yeah, real balmy," Mitch muttered. "I went to fill up the Jeep and practically froze to death."

Seth chuckled and followed him inside, calling out a greeting to his sister and Lauren. Lauren smiled and brushed a strand of silvery-blond hair back from her face. The elegant gesture only emphasized her cool beauty.

He pulled his attention from her and focused on the shop. For an older building, it was surprisingly warm. Seth unzipped his coat. It had been a week or so since he'd been inside. Even in that short time, he could see the improvements his sister had made.

He experienced a surge of pride. For years Anna had struggled to find her place in the world. But since she'd returned to Sweet River, she'd come into her own. She was happy now, content with her life. Everything she'd been searching for in Colorado she'd found on her return to the community where she'd grown up. She had a man she loved and now a thriving new business. It wouldn't surprise Seth if he'd be welcoming a new niece or nephew in the next year.

Yes, his sister had it all. The realization was bitter-sweet. He'd been in her position once. Three years ago he'd had a wife he loved. And, fool that he was, he'd taken that blessing for granted.

"Looks like the snow is really starting to fly," Anna said with a worried frown, her gaze settling on the melting flakes dripping from his boots onto the hardwood floor.

"The roads are okay for now." Mitch moved from the entryway to his wife's side, slipping an arm around her waist and brushing a kiss across her cheek. "But the sooner we get moving, the better."

Anna leaned against her husband with an intimacy that made Seth's chest tighten. She ignored her husband's subtle hint to hurry and instead shifted her gaze to Seth. "I learned something very interesting this evening."

Seth supposed he could ask what she'd learned. But from her expression she was going to tell him whether he asked or not.

"I invite you and Dani to spend Christmas Eve at my house. You turn me down. I tell you we'll come to your house. You say no." His sister's voice trembled with pent-up emotion. "Then I find out that not only are you spending the evening with Lauren, she's also spending the night at your house."

Seth clenched his jaw. He'd known he wouldn't be able to keep Lauren's visit quiet. That would be asking too much in a town the size of Sweet River. But he really hadn't wanted to deal with the issue tonight.

He shot a glance in Lauren's direction. She lifted one shoulder in a slight shrug. "Anna and I don't have any secrets."

"You dog." Mitch punched his arm. "You didn't tell me you and Lauren had hooked up."

Seth's spine went rigid. "We're—"

"We haven't hooked up," Lauren said with a dismissive wave. "Seth invited me to have dinner with him and Dani. I accepted. That's all."

"That's all?" The devilish gleam in Mitch's eyes was at odds with his innocent expression. "What about the sleepover?"

"You know how the roads are where I live." Seth met Mitch's gaze. "I have a perfectly good guest room. It seemed easier for Lauren to stay than to take her all the way home late at night."

"And this way I get to see Dani open her gifts," Lauren added.

"And I won't," Anna said.

Seth saw the disappointment in his sister's eyes. Heard it in her words. He swallowed a curse. He'd never intended to hurt Anna. Yet he had. And he understood why she was confused. On the surface the choices he'd made didn't make sense. Why *would* he invite Lauren and not his family?

The answer was impossible to share. How could he tell the bubbly bride that seeing her so happy and in love was like a knife to the heart, reminding him of what he'd once had and lost? He would not burden Anna with something that was his problem, his weakness.

Finding another woman and falling in love again would help fill the void in his life but that wasn't an option. He'd promised his wife on her deathbed that he wouldn't remarry until Dani was out of high school. And he was a man of his word.

Asking Lauren to join him and Dani had been a spur-of-the-moment action. He'd had second thoughts about the invitation almost as soon as the words left his mouth. Still, Dani had been thrilled when she'd learned Lauren would be joining them.

From the moment Lauren had set foot in Sweet River six months ago, his daughter had taken an instant liking to the beautiful professor.

"So what's the explanation?" Anna demanded when the silence lengthened. "Why didn't you want to spend Christmas with me?"

"You just got married." Seth picked up a pair of gloves from the display even as his gaze remained fixed on his sister. "I wanted you and Mitch to be able to enjoy the holiday without any family pressures."

It wasn't the whole truth but it was close enough. Though Anna and Mitch had delayed their wedding trip until March, they were technically still honeymooners.

"You know Seth loves you," Lauren said in a soft voice. "I'm sure he only wants what's best for you."

"Maybe. Let's say I believe you had my best interests at heart." Anna snatched the gloves from his hands and slapped them against the counter. "Next time you give me the choice."

He'd hurt her. He saw that now. He'd been so focused on his own needs that he'd failed to consider hers. "I'm sorry, Anna. If you and Mitch want to come over tonight—"

"We're celebrating with Mitch's family this evening," Anna said. "But we're free tomorrow."

Seeing the unsure look in her eyes only added to Seth's guilt. He smiled encouragingly. "Why don't you come over in the morning. You can watch Dani open her gifts, and we can all have lunch, maybe play some cards."

"C'mon, Anna, say yes," Lauren urged. "It'd be so much fun."

"It *would* be fun." Anna slanted a sideways glance at Mitch and he nodded. "What time?"

Seth thought for a minute. "Nine?"

"We'll be there," Anna said, the light back in her eyes.

Lauren squeezed Anna's arm. "I'm so happy you're coming."

Anna smiled. "Me, too."

Seth let his gaze linger on Lauren. She'd always been such a good, supportive friend to his sister. And she'd always gone out of her way to be nice to him. Any regret over his impromptu invitation disappeared. He was glad she'd be spending Christmas with him and Dani.

She caught him staring and smiled.

"Ready to go?" he asked. "I don't want to keep Connie away from her own family any longer than necessary."

Lauren grabbed her coat and bags from the counter. "We just need to stop by the house for my overnight bag."

Overnight. The impact of what he'd done struck him. A woman would be spending the night in his home. Not any woman, he clarified, *Dani's potential babysitter.* The tightness gripping his chest eased.

Lauren gave Mitch and then Anna a quick hug. "See you tomorrow."

The physical contact surprised him. He'd never thought of Lauren as the touchy-feely type. She'd always seemed more…businesslike.

Of course, she *had* hugged him in her kitchen only a few days earlier. The feel of her soft body pressed against him had brought all sorts of memories and feelings flooding back. Even though he'd told himself it was just a simple hug by his sister's friend, his body hadn't gotten the message. He was just relieved Lauren hadn't noticed.

"Are you feeling okay?"

Seth looked up to find Anna staring. "Why do you ask?"

"You look a little flushed."

He ran a finger along the inside collar of his coat. "That's because you keep it like an oven in here."

"Hot?" Mitch laughed. "Are you crazy? I can see my breath."

"Speaking of temperature…" Anna turned to Lauren. "If you get cold in his house, don't ask, just turn up the thermostat. My darling brother is like an Eskimo." Anna shook her head. "I practically have to wear my coat inside his home."

Granted Seth was most comfortable with the house cool, but Anna was exaggerating. "You didn't wear your jacket when you and Mitch stopped out a couple days ago."

"That's because Mitch was there to keep me warm." Anna cupped her husband's face with her hand and planted a lengthy kiss on his more-than-willing lips.

"Not warm. Hot." Mitch's hands slid sensuously up and down his wife's back. "I keep you hot."

"You most certainly do." Anna breathed a happy sigh before shifting her gaze back to Seth and Lauren. "That's another option for you."

"Option for what?" Lauren asked, looking perplexed.

Anna put her hands on her hips. "Must I spell everything out?"

The twinkle lurking in Anna's eyes sent red flags popping up. A shiver of unease skittered up Seth's spine. "That's okay—"

"Spell it out," Lauren said innocently, obviously not sensing the danger.

"Personal contact," Anna said. "Why worry about the thermostat when you have in your power the capability to generate your own heat?"

"Anna," Seth growled in warning.

"Are you suggesting I sleep with your brother?" Lauren sounded more amused than shocked.

"I'll leave the specifics to you." Anna's lips curved in a sly smile.

"You have gone too far," Seth said between gritted teeth. "To suggest—"

His words were drowned out by the sound of Lauren's laughter. "Thanks for the great advice, Anna. If I get cold I'll definitely consider your suggestion."

Chapter Three

Lauren gazed down at the Candyland game board spread out before her, the brightly colored spaces creating a cheery pattern on Seth's family room floor. As she prepared to take her turn, she wiped the beads of sweat from her brow. She couldn't believe Anna thought Seth kept his home too cool.

Pushing the sleeves of her sweater up to her elbows, Lauren removed the top card from the stack and flipped it over. Yellow. She moved her marker three steps forward to the next space of that color. Behind her a blazing fire crackled in the hearth. The buttery smell of the popcorn they'd eaten earlier in the evening still hung in the air.

After dinner, instead of playing the game at the table—as Lauren had expected—Seth had placed it on the floor in front of the fireplace. Then he'd used pillows to prop Dani up against the sofa right in front of the game. The proximity hadn't helped. With her right arm in a bright pink cast and her left leg in a plastic walker cast, Dani still needed help playing the game.

"Your turn." Seth picked up the stack of cards and held them out to his daughter. With her left hand, Dani flipped over the top card.

A huge smile spread across the child's face.

Seth glanced at the board and groaned loudly before moving her piece to the last rainbow space. He shifted his gaze to Lauren and heaved a dramatic sigh. "Can you believe she beat us again?"

"Super job, Dani." Lauren grinned. Competitive as she was, the look of pleasure on the little girl's face made losing painless. "You're definitely the Candyland Queen."

"I know I am," Dani said with childlike honesty. "Now I want to play Go Fish."

Lauren widened her eyes in mock surprise. "Go fishing? In this weather?"

Dani's giggles turned to peals of laughter. "It's a card game, silly."

"I don't think I've ever played it." Though she'd heard of it, there weren't many children's games Lauren *had* played. The day school she'd attended had been focused on academics, and her evenings had been filled with "enrichment" activities.

"I can teach you." Dani's voice quivered with excitement. "It's not hard. And it's really, really fun."

"You'll have to show her tomorrow." Seth glanced

at the clock on the wall as it began to chime. "It's nine o'clock and your bedtime. Tomorrow will be a big day."

The child's pout morphed into a smile. "I've been super-duper good this year." She leaned forward, resting her arm cast on the leg propped up on a pillow. "Santa is going to bring me lots and lots and lots of presents. Right, Daddy?"

Lauren sat back, curious how Seth would respond.

"I'm sure you'll get some," he said in a matter-of-fact tone. "But Santa will be stopping at the homes of many other children who've also been good. He has to have presents to give them, too."

Lauren shifted her gaze from Seth to Dani then back to Seth. Surely Dani didn't actually *believe* in Santa Claus. Lauren's parents had set her straight at a young age about the jolly bearded man, a figure perpetuated by advertising firms and retailers.

"I want to go to bed now," Dani announced. "'Cause if I'm not asleep, Santa won't stop."

Seth nodded his approval. "Did Mrs. Swenson help you wash up this evening?"

Dani nodded. "But I do have to go to the bathroom."

"I can take her," Lauren volunteered, not sure what helping would involve, but willing to try. After a delicious dinner of prime rib and mac 'n' cheese followed by three fast-paced games of Candyland, she was ready to stretch her legs.

"Thanks, but I've got it covered." Seth pushed to his feet, leaned over and lifted Dani into his arms then whinnied. "Hold on, cowgirl. The horsey is leaving the starting gate."

Lauren stared in awe as he galloped from the room. She couldn't imagine her father playing such a game with her. In fact, she couldn't remember her father ever even hugging her. He *had* shaken her hand when she'd graduated from college. And again when she'd earned her master's degree...

She shoved aside the memories and rose to her feet. By the time Seth trotted back to the living room with Dani, Lauren had finished her eggnog, put away the board game and returned the pillows to the sofa.

Seth smiled at Lauren as he settled Dani on the sofa. "I'll be right back."

He returned a moment later with a glass of milk, a plate of graham crackers and a container filled with assorted Christmas cookies. After removing the Tupperware lid, Seth carefully placed the container on Dani's lap then held out the plate.

Lauren stared with interest at the array of cookies. She couldn't believe they were going to eat more after the big dinner and popcorn they'd already consumed. "They look delicious but I don't think I can eat another bite."

"These aren't for us." Dani's fingers tightened around the lip of the container, as if fearful Lauren was going to snatch them away and gobble them down. "These are for Santa."

Dani selected three of the most brightly colored sugar ones and carefully placed them on the Christmas plate.

"He gets milk, too." Seth positioned the plate next to the glass on the table.

"And we put out extra for the reindeer," Dani added.

"Yep." Seth nodded, his lips quirking upward. "They have a lot of flying to do. They need to keep their energy up."

Lauren's smile froze on her face.

"Time for bed, kiddo." Seth scooped Dani into his arms. Though the plastic cast had a rocker ball so she could walk without putting pressure on the fractured leg, Seth had told Lauren that the doctor preferred Dani keep her weight off it for at least the next couple of days. "Tell Miss Lauren good-night."

Seth stepped closer and the exuberant seven-year-old surprised Lauren by flinging an arm around her neck and planting a big kiss on her cheek. "Thank you for coming and eating and playing Candyland with me."

Lauren gently smoothed a strand of hair back from the child's brow. With her blond curls tousled around her face, Dani looked like a little angel. "Merry Christmas, Danica."

"Merry Christmas to you, too," Dani called to Lauren as her father carried her from the room.

Since her injury, the child had been sleeping in the master bedroom on the main floor, while Seth had moved to the guest room. When he'd shown Lauren the bedrooms, he'd made it clear that if she did agree to move in, the guest room would be hers and he'd sleep in Dani's canopy bed.

The thought of the rugged cowboy in the tiny twin bed with its frilly pink-and-white bedspread brought a smile to Lauren's lips. As if her musings had conjured him up, Lauren heard the click of cowboy boots on hardwood. She turned to find Seth in the doorway, a satisfied smile on his face. "Surely she's not already asleep?"

"She's pretending to be," Seth said with a grin that caused her breath to catch in her throat. "She wants Santa to show up and knows he won't come until she's asleep."

The comment pulled her attention from his mouth. Though she told herself it didn't matter if his daughter believed in mythological figures and he indulged such thinking, the strange tension gripping her said somehow it *did* matter.

"Isn't Dani a little old to believe in Santa?" While it may have been a question, her tone made her feelings on the matter quite clear. And Lauren didn't stop there. She gestured to the plate of treats and the glass of milk. "And practices such as these just fuel the illusion."

The words hung in the air for a long moment. Lauren thought about calling them back. Though she'd meant what she'd said, she could have been more diplomatic.

To her surprise Seth didn't seem to take offense. In fact, by the twitch of his lips, you'd have thought she'd said something amusing. He reached over and grabbed two cookies from the plate, handing one to her and keeping the other for himself. "These *practices* are about embracing the magic of the season."

An illogical argument if she'd ever heard one, but charmingly delivered. Lauren took a bite of cookie and chewed for a moment. "Dani's a smart little girl. She can't really believe in elves and reindeer and Santa Claus."

"She seems to," Seth said, without a hint of embarrassment. "And as long as she does, I'm going to be supportive."

"Supportive? Of a lie?" Lauren wasn't sure what had gotten into her. Her training had taught her the importance of every word uttered. These outbursts weren't like her. But something about the whole Santa lie felt…personal.

Seth's brows pulled together and for a second he looked as if he might argue the point. But instead he shut his mouth and studied her for a long moment. "You never got to believe in Santa."

Instead of comforting her as perhaps he'd intended, the observation stirred up a hornet's nest of memories. Restless, she moved to the front window and, for several seconds, gazed out at the thick blanket of snow.

"My parents called him a bogus, fantasy figure," she said, turning back to face him. "A myth that contributed to the commercialization of Christmas."

"Did you ever go to a store and sit on his knee?" Seth asked, ignoring the outburst. "Whisper in his ear what you really wanted for Christmas?"

"Since he wasn't real, what would have been the point? Besides, it wouldn't have mattered," Lauren said with a sigh. "My parents didn't believe in giving gifts for Christmas. Still don't."

"Not at all?"

Lauren shook her head. "To them Christmas is just another federal holiday."

Seth hooked his thumbs in his front pockets and appeared to ponder her words. It took a moment before he spoke. "If you *could* have sat on Santa's knee and asked him for a gift when you were Dani's age, what would it have been?"

Lauren shifted her gaze, remembering back. "There

was only one thing I ever wanted for Christmas. That year I gathered my courage and approached my mother. I told her there was something I really, really wanted. I promised if she'd buy it for me I wouldn't ask for another gift *ever.*"

"What did she say?"

"She asked what it was. When I told her…she laughed." Lauren pressed her lips together, the long-ago hurt returning, squeezing her chest. She took a steadying breath. "Still, I went to bed that Christmas Eve hopeful. In the back of my little-girl mind, I thought this could be her chance, a way to show that she loved me. Crazy, huh?"

"Not crazy," Seth said softly. "Did she buy it for you?"

Not trusting her voice, Lauren shook her head.

"What had you asked for?"

"It doesn't matter." Lauren shifted her gaze away from those eyes that seemed to see too much. "It was silly."

Most men would have gratefully changed the subject. Actually most would never have pursued the topic. But she was beginning to realize Seth wasn't most men. So Lauren wasn't really surprised when he took her hand and tugged her to the sofa, dropping down to sit beside her. "Tell me."

His tone invited confidences. His eyes promised no matter what she said, *he* wouldn't laugh.

"A Cabbage Patch Kid." Lauren felt her cheeks warm. She lifted her chin. "They were extremely popular when I was in grade school. My friend Wendy had seven of them. You probably don't know what they are—"

"Spencer David."

"What?"

"Spencer David was Anna's Cabbage Patch doll. She got him when she was about Dani's age." A tiny smile lifted Seth's lips. "She took him everywhere she went. I remember one time…"

A dimple she never knew he possessed flashed in his left cheek.

"What?" Lauren touched his arm, the flannel of his shirt soft against her fingers. She immediately released her hold and let her hand drop to her side, but her heart still fluttered.

"We were at the rodeo. Anna was about to be crowned Little Miss Yellowstone County. When my parents went down to the arena to take pictures, they left Spencer with me." The dimple flashed again. "Just what every boy wants—to be at a public event with a doll by his side."

Lauren resisted the urge to smile at his pained expression. "I'm sure no one even noticed."

"No one except every friend I had, including Josh and Mitch." Seth rolled his eyes. "You can imagine the comments. Then Wes Danker came up with the brilliant idea of throwing Spencer David over the top rail into a pile of manure. The guys were all for it."

Lauren gasped. "Did you let him?"

"I couldn't," Seth said. "Anna would have been heartbroken. Not to mention mad as hell."

Something told Lauren it wasn't Anna's anger that had made him protect Spencer David as much as it was the knowledge of what that doll meant to his little sister. She wondered what it'd be like to have someone care about her that much. A lump formed in her throat but she swallowed past it. "You're a good person, Seth Anderssen."

"Naw, just watchin' out for my own hide." Seth stretched and covered a yawn. "Sorry. Dani's leg was bothering her and I hardly slept last night."

"We can call it an evening anytime you want." Lauren kept her tone light, not wanting him to see her disappointment. This had been the best Christmas Eve she could remember and she was reluctant to see it end. "I brought a book to read—"

"I'm not talking about going to bed right now," Seth said, looking startled. "I was just thinking it's time to start putting the presents under the tree."

Lauren shifted her gaze to the eight-foot Douglas fir that sat in front of the window. New and old ornaments intermingled on the thick bushy branches. Bubble lights had replaced traditional lighting. A unique tin-punched silver star that Seth had admitted making in middle school topped the tree.

Lauren had been so awed by the massive tree and its decorations that she hadn't noticed the lack of presents beneath its branches.

"I'll be happy to help." She glanced around. "Where are the gifts?"

"Hidden in one of the upstairs closets." Seth gestured with his head toward the stairs. "But you don't need to do a thing. I'll change and bring them down."

"Change?"

"Into the Santa suit." Though they were the only two in the room, Seth's voice dropped to a whisper. "I always wear it when putting the presents under the tree."

Lauren paused. "But this year is diff—"

"No different." A tiny muscle in Seth's jaw jumped.

Lauren wasn't about to argue. Only a few days ago Seth had faced the possibility of losing his daughter. Keeping to tradition was probably his way of reassuring himself that all was still well in his world.

"You might want to turn down the thermostat before you put on the suit." Her lips quirked upward. "Wouldn't want Santa to get a heatstroke."

"It is a little warm in here," Seth admitted.

An understatement if she'd ever heard one. Lauren chuckled. "Ya think?"

"I wanted to make sure you were comfortable." A swath of color cut across Seth's cheeks. "Guess I went a little overboard."

"Only by about a gazillion degrees." Lauren kept her tone light, ignoring the trickle of sweat slithering down her spine.

Seth rose and crossed the room to the thermostat. Almost immediately, the hot air that had been billowing out of the duct near the sofa stopped. "Better?"

"Much."

He smiled and started for the stairs, then stopped and turned back. "Can I get you anything before I go upstairs? More eggnog? Ice water? Glass of tea?"

"I'm fine," Lauren said, realizing she was more than fine. In fact, she couldn't remember the last time she'd felt so content. "I think I'll put in another Christmas CD. Set the stage for a visit from St. Nick."

"You're being awfully accommodating to the bogus, fantasy figure who contributes to the commercialization of Christmas," Seth teased.

Something about the way he said the words made Lauren grin. "Chalk it up to capturing some of that Anderssen Christmas spirit you've been dishing out in great abundance tonight."

"Good to hear." Seth smiled and her heart skipped a beat. "Back in five."

Lauren found herself humming as she searched through the stack of Christmas CDs. She finally settled on one that featured original artists performing their classic Christmas hits. After popping the disc into the sound system, Lauren turned down the volume before returning to her seat on the sofa.

Though the furnace had stopped pumping hot air, the temperature in the room was still in the sweltering range. Lauren considered her options. She could continue to suffer in silence or she could make a small wardrobe adjustment.

In a matter of seconds, her bulky sweater was up and over her head, leaving her cool and comfortable in the skimpy black tank she'd worn underneath.

With her body temperature now under control, Lauren leaned her head back against the top of the sofa, closed her eyes and let the strains of "White Christmas" wash over her.

She'd intended to relax and enjoy the music. But when she opened her eyes to the faint jingle of bells and saw all the brightly wrapped gifts at the base of the tree, she realized she must have fallen asleep.

Lauren shifted in her seat and found Seth—er, Santa—drinking the glass of milk Dani had set out for him. "Appears circling the world in a sleigh is thirsty business."

"It is indeed," Seth said, the fake white beard moving up and down as he spoke in his deep fake-Santa voice. "Delivering presents is very hard work."

Lauren studied him for a moment, then rose to her feet and strolled close. There was something about the suit that intrigued her. Perhaps it was the white fur trim on the coat. Or maybe the shiny black belt. Or the red hat with the pom-pom at the tip.

All she knew was she couldn't take her eyes off him—er, the suit. She resisted the urge to stroke the red velour and see if it really was as soft as it appeared. Because touching the fabric would mean touching Seth…

"Are there any lumps of coal for me under that tree?" Lauren asked abruptly.

"Not a single lump," he assured her, adding a very convincing "Ho-ho-ho." "I have it on good authority that Lauren Van Meveren has been a very good girl this year."

"I'm not sure your information is entirely accurate." Lauren inhaled the intoxicating scent of his cologne and took a step closer. She'd never been attracted to overweight, white-haired, bearded men before, but for some reason she found this one incredibly sexy.

And it appeared Santa wasn't immune to her charms. His gaze dropped to her shirt and she felt the tips of her breasts tighten.

As his gaze lingered, raw want coursed through her, igniting a need that shook her with its intensity. She couldn't recall the last time she'd craved a man's hands on her this badly.

The desire flickering in his suddenly dark eyes told

her Santa was having some naughty thoughts of his own. The realization gave her the courage she needed to wrap her arms around his neck. "I've always wanted to kiss a man with a beard."

Seth stiffened and for a second she worried she'd misread the signals. Then, without warning, his mouth closed over hers. His hands splayed against her back and he pulled her as close as his overstuffed belly would permit.

Waves of desire washed over Lauren and she gave in to the moment, until an excited voice cut through the passionate fog.

"Daddy, Daddy, come quick!" Dani called from the doorway. "Santa is kissing Miss Lauren!"

Chapter Four

Seth wrenched himself out of Lauren's arms and raced for the stairs, his stuffed belly jiggling like a bowl full of jelly. Out of the corner of his eyes he caught a glimpse of Dani's face. Mouth open. Eyes wide.

Four steps up was all it took for Seth to lasso in his rioting emotions. Running wasn't the answer. There was a child—his child—to consider. He rested a white-gloved hand on the rail, turned and let loose his best "Ho-ho-ho!" before continuing heartily, "Danica Sue Anderssen, Santa hopes you like your gifts. You've been a very good girl this year."

Warmth rushed through him at the look of pleasure that flushed his daughter's face.

"I have been good, Santa." Dani's words tumbled out

one after the other. "My daddy says I'm the best girl ever."

Not sure how to respond, Seth gave another, "Ho-ho-ho!"

He realized he should have thought of something better when Dani's eyes darted around the room. "Where *is* Daddy?"

"He went upstairs." Lauren's voice was calm and serene.

If the kiss had affected her, it certainly didn't show. Seth wasn't sure why the thought brought a surge of disappointment.

"Daddy! Daddy!" Dani bellowed, her tone reverberating with excitement. "Come see who's here!"

Lauren's gaze met his, her green eyes piercing.

Go. Go. Go.

Across the distance, the unspoken words slapped Seth in the face, rousing him to action.

"The reindeer are restless," Seth said in his deepest Santa voice. "We've many stops still to make. I thank you for the cookies and milk. And the reindeer thank you, too."

Without saying another word, Seth whirled and raced up the stairs. By the time he reached the guest room, the Santa suit was almost off. In record time the beard was discarded and the suit and accessories back in the closet.

Dressed now in the jeans and shirt he'd worn underneath, Seth took a deep steadying breath. He could do this. He *had* to do this. There was no way he was going to let an impulsive action steal his daughter's innocent belief in Santa.

With that thought firmly in front of him, Seth sauntered down the stairs as if he hadn't a care in the world. When he saw Dani seated on the sofa next to Lauren, his heart slammed against his ribs. So much hinged on how he handled these next few minutes. Calling upon the acting experience gleaned from several high school plays, Seth forced what he hoped could pass for an excited expression. "Did you see Santa?"

"I saw him." Dani bounced up and down on the sofa. "I saw him kissing Miss Lauren."

Seth had never blushed in his life but at that moment he came pretty darn close. Somehow he managed to meet Lauren's gaze. "You were kissing Santa?"

Even to his own ears, his shock sounded genuine.

"Guilty as charged." Lauren lifted a hand, the twinkle in her eyes taking him by surprise. "I gave him a friendly kiss to say thanks for stopping by."

"It was like the kisses Aunt Anna gives Uncle Mitch when they're in the kitchen alone," Dani said in a loud voice. "She had her arms around him and everything."

Seth closed his eyes. Dear God, could this get any worse? He opened his eyes a second later to the sound of Lauren's laughter.

"What can I say? I was swept away. The old bearded guy knows how to kiss." Lauren shot him a wink.

Though Seth told himself it shouldn't matter what Lauren thought of his kissing ability, his chest puffed with pride. If he was being honest, he'd admit that for a second, he'd been swept away, too. He'd forgotten how good it felt to hold a woman. How good it felt to have soft, warm lips pressed against his. Most of all, how good it felt to simply be that close to another human being.

The three years since Jan passed had been lonely ones. Oh, he kept busy raising Dani and running the ranch. He played ball with his friends and went to church with his neighbors. But he hadn't realized until now how much he missed physical intimacy.

"What happened to Santa, Daddy?" Dani's sweet voice broke through his thoughts. "Where did he go?"

"Out the bedroom window," Seth said. "The reindeer were pawing the roof. I'm surprised you didn't hear them. I think they were eager to deliver more presents."

Dani's mouth formed a perfect *O*. "Did you see them? Did you see *Rudolph?*"

"Yes, Seth," Lauren asked, her lips twitching. "Was Rudolph with them?"

"Everything happened so fast." Though it seemed weird to be having a conversation about a *reindeer,* Seth somehow managed to keep a straight face. "I'm afraid I didn't look for him."

Dani exhaled a heavy sigh. "I wish I could have seen Rudolph and the other reindeer."

"Me, too." Lauren reached over and gave Dani a sympathetic hug. "At least we got to see Santa."

Lauren's generosity of spirit toward his daughter continued to amaze him.

"When I heard bells jingling, I knew it was Santa," Dani said to Lauren, her expression oh-so-earnest. "That's why I got out of bed."

"I don't blame you," Lauren responded.

Seth stared in amazement.

Lauren's expression was as serious as his daughter's. Despite the psychologist's feelings about fantasy figures, she seemed determined to help him preserve Dani's innocence.

"Since Santa was here already, can I open my presents now?" Dani's focus shifted to the stack of brightly wrapped gifts beneath the tree. "Pretty, pretty, pretty please?"

When his daughter turned her attention back to Seth, her blue eyes shining with hope, he wanted to give her the world. Only the thought of his sister stopped him. Anna and Mitch were coming over tomorrow specifically to share Christmas morning with their niece. He could imagine how they'd feel if they arrived and found gifts already opened. "'Fraid not, princess."

"Please, Daddy, please," Dani begged.

"Just think, once your aunt Anna gets here tomorrow, you get to open Santa's gifts *and* the ones from her and your uncle Mitch," Lauren said soothingly.

Seth pretended not to notice Dani's trembling lower lip. Experience had taught him that commenting on her distress would only make things worse. Instead he moved to the sofa and lifted her high over his head, careful not to bang her casts. "Can you see Rudolph from way up there?"

Dani giggled. "He's not here, silly."

The childish laughter was music to his ears. As Seth lowered his arms and hugged her close, he was struck by how much of Jan lived in her. Dani had her mom's button nose, curly hair and crooked smile. And from the moment she was born, she'd had her mother's total and complete love.

Growing up, Jan had experienced firsthand the disaster that sometimes happens when a parent remarries. During those last weeks of life she'd worried that her daughter would experience that same pain. Assuring her that he wouldn't remarry until Dani was out of high school had been a small price to pay to ease her fears.

The promise had been freely given and would be kept. The only problem was that Seth hadn't foreseen the loneliness of a single-parent existence. Hadn't fully taken into account his physical needs. His friend Wes Danker had once said that if he had an itch, he scratched it. But Wes wasn't a father. Seth couldn't just go out and have a brief fling. Not in Sweet River. Not without causing talk.

He remembered how hard such gossip had been on Mitch growing up. Seth would never put Dani in such a position.

"Good night, Dani...again." Lauren stood and leaned close, brushing her lips across the child's forehead. "Sweet dreams."

"You smell good." Dani studied Lauren. "And you're very pretty. I bet that's why Santa kissed you."

A swath of red cut across Lauren's cheeks.

Dani squirmed in Seth's arms so she could look up at him. "You think she's pretty and smells good, don't you, Daddy?"

Seth gave a noncommittal smile. He'd noticed the sultry scent that wafted about Lauren, a scent that stirred his senses. And pretty? No living, breathing man could say otherwise. But this was his sister's friend, his daughter's potential babysitter. Although kissing her had probably been a mistake, he wasn't going to compound the error by saying sweet words that might give her the wrong impression.

He'd been under the influence of the Santa suit when he'd lost control. Which meant that as long as he steered clear of red velour and hats with pom-poms, he should be safe.

A wave of irritation washed over Lauren. She'd felt sure that Santa—er, Seth—had noticed her new perfume, but for some reason he refused to admit it. Six months ago she'd have been devastated if Seth had disavowed any attraction to her. But that was when she'd had a silly crush on him, one more suitable to a schoolgirl than a mature, educated woman.

The "crush" period had begun shortly after she'd moved to Sweet River. She'd never been around a rugged cowboy before. And Seth had been so helpful in getting her settled. When he found out she needed single male subjects for her research project, he'd made it a personal goal to recruit the men.

For some reason, and perhaps it had been a reaction to the testosterone and kindness, she'd gone off the deep end, getting all nervous and excited whenever he was around. Then one day, she'd overheard him asking Anna to quit trying to hook him up with her friends. Though his tone had been joking, Lauren had realized how ridiculous she'd been acting. And, even if he had been interested in her, this was a man who could never be more than a friend. He was a rancher who loved his home and his life in Montana. She was an academician with her sights set on tenure at an Ivy League college.

Still, the attraction lingered. Though she wasn't sure

he felt it, there had been electricity in the air whenever they were in the same room. It wasn't until the steamy dreams started that she finally realized it was a *physical* attraction drawing her to Seth.

Just like tonight. The Kiss—it had somehow achieved capitalized status in her mind—had been a purely physical response to the chemistry between them. It had nothing to do with the fact that they shared an interest in the writings of Thoreau, or both loved old horror movies. And the kindness he displayed toward his daughter—and to her—hadn't factored into the equation at all.

"It was lust, pure and simple," Lauren advised the fireplace, giving her head a decisive nod.

"What was lust?"

Apparently while she wasn't looking, Seth had returned to the room after putting Dani back to bed. He dropped into the chair next to the sofa where Lauren sat.

"The Kiss," she said matter-of-factly. "What we experienced was simply a momentary lapse into lust."

She could tell she'd surprised him by speaking so frankly, but knew he'd understand. After all, he'd been gripped by the same fierce physical need. Lauren had felt it in the urgency of his lips, had seen it in the fire that had burned in his blue eyes.

"That kiss—" Seth raked a hand through his hair before continuing "—was a mistake."

"I disagree."

After shooting her an incredulous glance, Seth jerked to his feet and began to pace. "How can you think otherwise? My daughter saw you kissing me—I mean Santa Claus. She'll probably be traumatized for life."

Lauren rolled her eyes. She couldn't help it. She'd never seen anyone make such a big deal out of something that was no big deal. "On the list of things with potential to wound a child's psyche, seeing your aunt's friend kissing Santa Claus wouldn't even make the top ten thousand."

His lips quirked upward. "Tell me if you think I'm overreacting."

"You're overreacting."

Seth laughed then stopped himself. He glanced in the direction of Dani's room. "Let's take this into the kitchen. We can talk more comfortably in there. I'll make some hot cocoa."

"Hot cocoa sounds good." Realizing that he was concerned about Dani overhearing their conversation, Lauren rose to her feet and stretched. "Especially if you have marshmallows."

Seth unexpectedly grinned. "I've got a whole bag."

His smile brought the desire surging back and Lauren was forced to concede it might not be the Santa suit after all. It appeared to be the man *in* the suit who'd hot-wired her synapses.

Seth didn't say a word on the short walk to the kitchen. Lauren hoped some hot cocoa and a whole lot of marshmallows would help him put The Kiss in proper perspective.

When they got to the kitchen, Lauren took a seat at the table while Seth pulled out a teakettle from the cupboard, filled it with water and placed it on one of the gas burners.

Lauren shot a quick glance at the microwave, reassuring herself that he did indeed have the appliance.

"Seth." Lauren leaned back in her chair. "Is your microwave broken?"

"Works fine." He stopped scooping cocoa into two Christmas mugs and looked up. "Why do you ask?"

"Just wondering why you're heating the water on the stove instead of in the microwave." Lauren forced herself to sound as nonjudgmental as possible. "I don't know anyone who uses teakettles anymore."

Seth's gaze shifted to the stove and a look she couldn't decipher crossed his face. "Jan always used one," he said finally. "She loved the way they whistled. She said it was such a happy sound. Even when she was dying, if I put on the teakettle, she—" Seth stopped and cleared his throat. "I use it in the winter because the house gets dry. It does a good job of putting humidity back into the air."

Anna had mentioned her sister-in-law had died from an aggressive form of breast cancer. That was the extent of what Lauren knew about the woman.

"Jan was your wife." Lauren said it as a statement of fact rather than a question. "Anna mentions her from time to time."

Seth nodded, but was saved from saying more when the kettle began to whistle.

"I can help." Lauren rose from her seat at the kitchen table as she spoke.

Seth waved her back down. "Under control."

Lauren waited until he'd taken his seat, the mugs before them filled with rich hot chocolate topped with several fluffy marshmallows, before she returned to the topic. "Tell me about your wife," she urged in a soft, low voice that encouraged confidences. "Tell me about Jan."

Seth took a sip of cocoa, his gaze watchful. "What do you want to know?"

"I didn't have the pleasure of meeting her," Lauren said. "I'd like you to share things that will help me get to know her."

"Why are you interested?" he asked, his tone more curious than resistant.

"You and Dani are my friends," Lauren said. "And if I do end up caring for your daughter, knowing something about her mother would be beneficial."

"Makes sense," Seth grudgingly agreed. He took a sip of cocoa then placed his mug on the table. "Jan grew up on a ranch, just outside Sweet River. I knew her my whole life. She was a homebody. She loved to cook, sew and quilt. In fact, she was making a quilt for Dani when she died. She thought she'd get it finished but—"

He pushed back his chair with a clatter and jerked to his feet. "I forgot the cookies."

The last thing Lauren wanted was more food but she let him go, pretending she hadn't seen the tears in his eyes. She leaned back in her chair, sipping her hot cocoa while he grabbed the plastic container of cookies from the counter. His bootheels clacked on the hardwood as he returned to the table and plopped the container between them.

"Have one." He dropped into a chair and shoved the container closer. The eyes that met hers were clear and very blue.

Though she knew he'd used the cookies as a distraction, Lauren's mouth began to water as she gazed at all the varieties. She took a cookie…just to be polite. As she downed a clumsily decorated—yet still delicious—Nutter-Butter-Santa, she waited for Seth to continue his story. She waited. And waited. And waited.

Lauren didn't relish playing twenty questions but it appeared she had no choice. She wanted to learn more about Seth's wife. Not because she was nosy, but because losing a mother at such a young age was hard on a child. Understanding the dynamics of the family relationship would help her better meet Dani's needs. Okay, and maybe assuage her curiosity at the same time.

"Did you two go to the same college?" she finally asked. Anna had told him Seth had graduated from Central Montana University in Bozeman.

"Jan didn't attend college," he replied.

Lauren quirked a brow.

"Higher education wasn't her thing." Seth shrugged. "She was smart, but it was things around the house that interested her."

There were lots of arguments Lauren could have used, even the simple "education for the sake of education," but she stifled the urge. Why Jan had chosen not to pursue a degree was none of Lauren's business. "If she didn't go to college, what did she do after high school?"

"She worked at Millsteads' dude ranch." Seth's eyes took on a distant glow. "Jan was quite the history buff. She made meals for the tourists the old-fashioned way, in those big cast-iron skillets. Taught them how to make bread and soap the way the settlers did in the 1870s."

Lauren heard the pride in his voice, saw it in his eyes. "Sounds like an incredible woman."

"Jan always knew exactly what she wanted out of life." A smile lifted the corners of Seth's lips. "She was a great wife and mother."

Lauren felt a twinge of envy. The more he shared, the more it became clear that if Seth ever remarried that woman would have some pretty big shoes to fill.

"I'm not saying she was perfect," Seth added as if he could read her thoughts. "The fact that she always knew what she wanted sometimes made it hard for her to understand those of us who weren't so sure."

Lauren's ears pricked up. Seth had experienced career indecision?

"I struggled with what I wanted to be when I was growing up," Lauren said as she drew an imaginary figure eight on the tabletop with her finger, remembering the strained silence that would fill the house whenever she suggested something that didn't meet with her parents' approval. "I remember one time…I mentioned to my father I was considering getting a business degree and going into market research. He didn't speak to me for days."

"Yeah, right. No one would—" Seth stopped. "You're serious."

Lauren nodded.

"No offense to your dad, but what's wrong with that career?"

"Not prestigious enough. My father is a world-renowned mathematician. To him, market research is more art than science," Lauren said. "More important, it wasn't a field he'd chosen for me. Right off that made it unacceptable."

"Nice guy."

"I ended up falling in love with psychology. He liked that even less, but I let him rant." Lauren smiled. "What about your parents? Would they have been okay with you becoming something other than a rancher?"

Seth thought for a moment. "I think so."

"But ranching was in your blood." Lauren kept her tone light. "Right?"

"The land, this part of the country, is a part of me. But I struggled with the expectation that I would become a full-time rancher." The distant look returned to Seth's eyes. "From the time I was Dani's age, I wanted to be a large-animal vet."

"Why didn't you do it?" Responding to the passion in his voice, Lauren pushed her cup aside. She leaned forward and rested her elbows on the table.

"I was actually in my third year of vet school when my father started having health issues. Then he and my mother decided to move to Florida right around the time Jan discovered she was pregnant. It was clear my place was here, not in Bozeman."

"I didn't know you were married in college." Lauren wondered how she could have missed that part of the story.

"We were dating but not married." Seth's voice was even and well controlled. His expression gave nothing away. "Jan had some health concerns early in the pregnancy. She wasn't keen on being away from her folks. When my parents decided to relocate, it made sense for me to move back."

"But you only had a couple years left." Lauren did her best to hide her shock. "You gave up your dream when you were so close...."

"I suppose that's one way to look at it," Seth said. "I prefer to view it as trading one dream for another. Jan and Dani and the land were what I wanted, too."

Lauren stared in amazement. There wasn't an ounce of bitterness or regret in Seth's voice. Jan had been one lucky woman.

"Enough about me," Seth said with a dismissive wave. "Tell me about you."

Though she'd barely scratched the surface on what made Seth tick, his tone made it clear he wouldn't welcome any more questions about himself. In fact, she got the distinct impression he regretted saying as much as he had.

"Not much to tell." Lauren thought for a moment. "I already told you about my parents' commuter marriage and their commitment to their careers. They weren't planning on children, but my mom's IUD failed. She made sure they wouldn't be surprised again. She had her tubes tied right after I was born."

Seth's gaze searched her face. "Unexpected or not, they must be very proud of you."

"They have pretty high standards." Lauren spoke evenly, ignoring the dagger of pain lancing her heart. According to her parents she'd done a lot of things right and more than a few wrong. They hadn't understood why she'd pursued her PhD on a part-time basis instead of hitting it full-time. But teaching at the community-college level for several years had honed her classroom presentation skills and counseling patients had broadened her appreciation for the knowledge gained in her doctoral studies.

"From your description, I get the feeling they aren't

the kind who'd approve of you taking six weeks out of your life to babysit Dani," Seth said, filling the silence that draped over the table like a shroud.

"That's a major understatement." Lauren couldn't help but smile. Her father, Dr. Edmund Van Meveren, would be horrified his daughter would consider becoming anyone's live-in babysitter. Her mother, the prominent physicist Dr. Margaret King-Van Meveren, would find the whole situation unworthy of discussion. "But no worries. They haven't influenced my decisions in a very long time."

Seth's gaze lingered for a long moment. "Have you thought any more about watching her?"

Lauren opened her mouth, but Seth raised a hand before she could speak. "If you're not ready, don't feel obliged to answer. After Christmas is what we agreed upon. I can wait another couple days if you need more time."

"I've been thinking all evening," Lauren admitted. "Until you mentioned it over dinner, I hadn't realized that the school district would be sending out a teacher to work with Dani. Between you being home in the evening and the hours she'll spend with the teacher, I should have the time I need to work on my research and give Dani the time and attention she deserves."

Hope flared in Seth's eyes. "Are you saying you'll do it?"

"Congratulations, Mr. Anderssen." Lauren extended her hand. "You've got yourself a temporary nanny."

Chapter Five

Lauren rolled over in bed and pulled the covers tight around her shoulders. She kept her eyes closed, determined to fall back asleep. She'd been having such a pleasant dream about Seth. One that made her body feel all warm and tingly inside.

But the light streaming through the frosted windows and the smell of fresh coffee and frying bacon tugged at her. Reluctantly she opened one eye and glanced over at the clock.

Nine o'clock.

Anna and Mitch were probably already downstairs. Lauren jerked upright, her heart going from 60 to 100 in 3.5 seconds. Throwing off the warmth of the down comforter, she swung her legs over the side of the bed, ignoring the goose bumps popping up on her arms.

With her heart pounding, Lauren quickly showered and dressed. Figuring she was already late, she took an extra second to dab on some lip color, mascara and a spritz of perfume. Pulling her still-damp hair back with a couple of clips, she scampered down the steps.

Instead of waiting for her in the kitchen, Seth and Dani were in the living room. Though she was only wearing jeans and a fuzzy aqua-colored sweater that was more comfortable than fashionable, the look in Seth's eyes told her if this were baseball, she'd have hit a home run.

Lauren floated down the last couple of steps.

"Good morning." Seth's smile was warm and welcoming. "The bacon is cooked. I just need to know how you like your eggs."

"Daddy said we can't open presents until after we eat," Dani said with a petulant pout. "And he wouldn't wake you up."

Lauren felt the heat creep up her neck. Though there'd been no censure in Seth's eyes, he probably thought she was a total sloth. She was always talking about the long hours she worked, yet the first opportunity he'd had to observe her behavior she'd slept half the morning away. "I'm sorry. I'm not used to staying up so late."

It was a poor excuse, but the truth. She and Seth had sat in front of the fireplace, drinking the bottle of wine she'd brought over and talking until after one in the morning. Though he hadn't had the chance to travel like she had, he was well read and knew more than she did about many of the places she'd visited over the years.

"No problem," Seth said in a reassuring tone. "It was hard for me to get out of bed, too."

"Not me," Dani piped up, shifting slowly due to the cast on her leg. "I was up before Mr. Doodle-Do."

Lauren lifted a brow.

Seth grinned. "Dani has an alarm clock shaped like a rooster."

"I've had it a long time," Dani said loudly. "I was only five when Aunt Anna gave it to me."

"That was a long time ago." Lauren hid a smile. To a seven-year-old, two years probably did seem like an eternity.

"I thought we'd eat in the kitchen," Seth said, "then come back and open presents in here."

Lauren paused. "But what about Anna and Mitch? Shouldn't we wait for them?"

Seth turned with Dani now in his arms. "They called this morning."

"They're not coming." Dani's lips turned downward and her voice was heavy with disappointment.

"Did something happen?" Lauren couldn't imagine what it could be, but it had to be bad for Anna to forfeit Christmas with her niece.

"They're stuck," Dani volunteered. "Uncle Mitch is stuck in the snow."

"Is that true?" Lauren turned to Seth.

"There's a good amount of snow out there," Seth said. "From the sound of it, the foothills got even more than we did. Mitch was blading his lane and got stuck."

"Daddy told Uncle Mitch he needed to put chains on the tires." Dani seemed eager to share every detail of the conversation.

"It's easy to forget how hard this snow can be to plow."

"So they're not coming at all?" Lauren couldn't keep the disappointment from her voice. She'd been looking forward to sharing Christmas with her best friend.

"Doesn't sound like it," Seth said and continued quickly, "Now, I don't know about you, but I'm ready for some breakfast."

Dani tugged at her father's sweater. "Then can we open presents?"

"Yes, princess." Seth smiled. "Then we'll open presents."

The sun hung low in the sky and the interior of the older home had taken on a slight chill. Lauren twisted her new sterling silver bracelet back and forth around her wrist and waited for Seth to fetch her and Dani for their next adventure. He'd told them he had a surprise but refused to tell them the plans. Though his daughter had tried to wheedle it out of him, Lauren hadn't bothered. Whatever it was, she was confident she was going to like it. After all, the whole day had been one wonderful adventure after another.

The breakfast Seth had fixed had been magnificent. Lauren couldn't remember the last time she'd tasted orange juice from the carton so sweet or eaten bacon so perfectly crisp.

Opening presents had been hilarious—with Dani declaring each gift to be her favorite—as well as touching because of the child's delight and appreciation for everything she received. She'd loved the pink heart necklace Lauren had given her and insisted on putting it on the moment it was out of the gift sack.

After all Dani's gifts were open, Lauren expected

Seth to take center stage. But he told her it was tradition that gifts were opened by age—from youngest to oldest—and since she was younger than him, she would go next. Lauren had been struck dumb. Didn't he realize there were no gifts for her to open?

But, before she could figure out how to gracefully remind him of that fact, Dani had reached under the tree and pulled out two packages. The first present had been a Christmas mug filled with Hershey's Kisses. Lauren had immediately popped a couple in her mouth and then raved about the cup and the chocolates. Dani had beamed. The second gift had been a silver bracelet from Seth.

Lauren swallowed hard against the lump in her throat. When she'd opened the box and saw the bracelet nestled inside, she hadn't known what to say. The bracelet was perfect—delicate, classy, just the type she'd have chosen for herself.

The rest of the day had flown by. Between baking Kringles for the neighbors—another tradition—and Seth teaching her how to roast chestnuts in the fireplace, Lauren had been so busy she'd barely thought about her family. Only after both Stacie and Anna had called to wish them a merry Christmas did it hit Lauren that she hadn't heard from her parents.

But she shoved aside the hurt and told herself it didn't matter. She was going on another adventure. And, after a brief afternoon nap, she felt up to whatever Seth had planned. As he'd instructed, she and Dani were dressed in their warmest clothes.

"Daddy says this is a special surprise," Dani said from her spot in the living room. Her voice quivered with excitement as her uninjured leg swung back and forth. "Can you see him? What's he doing?"

Lauren moved to the window and pushed back the draperies. She pressed close to the glass but the windows were so frosty, it was impossible to see out. "I can't see much except snow."

After dumping a foot of the white stuff last night, the storm had moved out of the area, leaving behind a winter wonderland. The snow in the yard surrounding the ranch house glistened like a thousand diamonds.

The front door was flung open with a clatter. "Are you ready?"

"We're ready." Lauren stepped away from the window. Since he'd told them to dress warm, Lauren had put Dani in her new snowsuit. Thankfully Grandma Anderssen had bought it extra big. Though she knew they wouldn't be going on a hike, Lauren had even put a boot on Dani's uninjured leg.

For herself, Lauren had been forced to improvise. Because her coat was lightweight, she'd tried to layer. And, she told herself, at least she had warm boots.

Seth's gaze swept over his daughter, and he nodded his approval. But when he turned to Lauren, his brows pulled together. "That coat doesn't look like it would keep you warm on a day that was fifty and sunny."

"It's all I have." Lauren lifted her chin, wishing she'd gone for substance, rather than style, when choosing a coat to wear to Seth's house. "I put a long-sleeved tee under my sweater, so I should be good."

"I don't think so." With a determined expression, Seth reached past her and opened the closet door. He rummaged around, finally pulling out a thick dark gray coat with a hood. It reminded Lauren of one you'd wear in Maine on a moose hunt. Or in Montana doing…something. "You can borrow this one."

Seth held the coat out to her. After hanging up her jacket, Lauren slipped her arms into the sleeves and Seth pulled the coat around her and zipped it up. A faint woodsy scent of cologne clung to the lining and teased her nostrils.

"This will keep you warm." He flipped up the hood over the pastel-striped stocking cap Anna had given to her and tied it securely under her chin. Then he grabbed a scarf from the closet and looped it loosely around her neck. "Now you're ready to go."

"Where are we headed?" Lauren chuckled. "The North Pole?"

Dani, looking like a little Eskimo on the settee, giggled. "I want to go to there and see the elves."

Seth smiled mysteriously and opened the front door with a flourish. "Ladies, your carriage awaits."

Lauren stepped onto the front porch. Her breath caught in her throat at the sight of the old-fashioned sleigh. Small and compact with tufted upholstery, the wood body was the same rich burgundy as the seats. Several cream-colored stripes painted on the glossy side accentuated the deep color. Lauren was so enamored with the sleigh that it took her a couple seconds to notice the beautiful horse hitched to the front.

Held tightly in her father's arms, Dani clapped her hands, the sound muffled by her mittens. "Hooray! We get to go on a sleigh ride!"

Lauren turned to Seth. "I've seen these in old movies, but I never thought they still existed."

Seth smiled. "Are you up for a ride?"

"Are you kidding? Of course I am." Lauren started toward the steps, but was stopped by Seth's hand on her arm.

"Wait here. I'll get Dani settled and then I'll help you. The steps are icier than they look."

Though the air was brisk, warmth flowed through Lauren. She'd grown up in an egalitarian household where her father wouldn't presume to take care of her mother. Still, Lauren had to admit that Seth's solicitude made her feel special. She understood this behavior was just the Montana way. Men here were taught from a young age to take care of women. It wasn't anything personal. Yet somehow Seth's chivalrous behavior felt very personal.

"Ready to go?"

Lauren lifted her gaze. When Seth held out a hand, she realized with a surge of pleasure that he was wearing the gloves she'd given him for Christmas. She placed her hand in his and smiled. "Let the adventure begin."

Chapter Six

Seth slowed the sleigh to a stop in front of the Nordstrom ranch house and his Christmas spirit took a dip. This year there was no lighted star at the top of the stable. Because there was no one left who cared enough to put it there. His neighbor and friend Lars Nordstrom had passed away shortly before Thanksgiving. The home was now occupied by the rancher's son, Adam, who had arrived last week to settle the estate.

Though they hadn't run with the same crowd, Seth remembered the math genius from high school. Back then Seth had been into rodeo, sports and girls, not necessarily in that order. Adam had been more of an intellectual who'd made no secret of his hatred for all things Montana. It hadn't surprised anyone that once

Adam had left Sweet River for college, he'd rarely returned.

The barking of Old Ben, Lars's golden retriever, must have alerted Adam he had visitors because the light flipped on before Seth had even gotten out of the sleigh.

A man dressed in khakis, a navy sweater and an open ski jacket stepped onto the porch. Tall and lean with a messy mop of dark hair and thin wire-rimmed glasses, Adam looked very much the up-and-coming college professor.

Definitely Lauren's type.

Seth's hands tightened on the reins. "Merry Christmas, Adam. We brought you Kringle."

"Kringle?" The professor's serious expression eased into a smile. "That's always a welcome gift."

Adam's reaction was just what Seth had expected. There wasn't a person alive who didn't like the buttery, layered, almond-filled pastry. And Jan's recipe was the best. Although many traditionalists insisted Kringle be shaped like a pretzel, his wife had always made hers in an oval to eliminate the unfilled, overlapping parts.

For years, Seth had helped Jan make the pastry for friends and neighbors. Though the skill was usually passed from mother to daughter, Dani would have to learn from him. It was important to him that his child embrace her Norwegian heritage.

Today's lesson had gone surprisingly well. Dani had been an apt pupil. It helped that she and Lauren had learned together. In fact, having Lauren there had made the lesson more fun for all of them, Seth included.

"Come inside." Adam approached the sleigh. "Warm up. Have a cup of coffee and some Kringle with me."

Seth hesitated. It was almost Dani's bedtime. Still, he didn't want to be rude. And this *was* their last stop. He turned around to where Lauren sat with Dani on the backseat of the sleigh. His eyes locked with hers and for a second the world tilted sideways. It was the same craziness that had been happening all day.

Electricity sizzled in the air whenever he glanced her way. Desire shot through him like a bull out of a chute every time her hand brushed his. He wasn't sure why any of this was happening. It was damned annoying.

Lauren's voice broke through his thoughts. "A cup of anything hot sounds good to me."

"You can put the horse and sleigh in the stable, if you'd like." Adam gestured toward the building Seth had helped Lars shingle just last summer. "It's empty now so there's plenty of room."

Seth inhaled sharply. "You got rid of Hoss?"

Adam's head cocked. "Boss?"

"Hoss. The palomino," Seth said impatiently. Didn't he even know the name of the aging gelding that had been Lars's pride and joy?

A light of recognition flashed in Adam's eyes before he chuckled. "It wouldn't surprise me if that one was already at the glue factory."

Seth bit back a harsh reply. Hoss may have been long in the tooth but he had many good years left in him. And the horse had been more than a means of transportation—he'd been the lonely man's friend. Adam would have known that if he'd visited his dad more than once every five years.

Of course, even if Adam had been aware of the fact, it might not have made a difference to him. While Lars loved all living creatures, his son had never cared about the animals or the ranch. Seth settled his gaze on the well-kept house. It was difficult knowing that everything Lars had worked so hard to build, everything that he'd cared so much about, would be sold off piece by piece. Seth forced the depressing thought aside. The ranch was Adam's now, to do with as he wished.

The wind kicked up from the north. Out of the corner of his eye, Seth saw Dani duck her head and cuddle close to Lauren. Guilt clogged his throat. Worrying about Hoss and Lars's legacy was no excuse for neglecting his responsibilities.

Seth hopped to the ground. "Let's get inside where it's warm."

"I'd forgotten how cold it gets here." Adam zipped his coat before moving to the side of the sleigh and smiling at Lauren. "I don't believe we've met. I'm Adam Nordstrom."

The professor extended his hand and when it closed over Lauren's bulky mittened one, Seth saw the interest on Adam's face. For a second Seth was seized with the urge to tell the professor to keep his coffee, that they were heading straight home. Thankfully he reined in his caveman protective instincts just in time.

"Adam, this is Anna's friend Lauren Van Meveren." Seth shifted his gaze to Lauren. "Adam and I went to high school together. Nordstroms have owned this land since the 1800s."

Lauren stepped from the sleigh, her hand still in Adam's. "Pleased to meet you, Mr. Nordstrom."

"Likewise, Miss Van Meveren."

"Call me Lauren," she said with a smile.

"Only if you call me Adam," he immediately countered.

"Deal," Lauren said.

Seth resisted the urge to gag at the sophomoric repartee.

Adam cocked his head and studied Lauren for several seconds. "I know this is a long shot, but are you any relation to Dr. Edmund Van Meveren at Stanford?"

"He's my father," Lauren said without hesitation, but Seth noticed her smile didn't quite reach her eyes. "Do you know him personally? Or from his work?"

"Both." Adam's expression grew animated. "I was his teaching assistant when I was working on my PhD in Applied Mathematics. The man is absolutely brilliant. I'm now teaching at Brown, but I've continued to follow his achievements."

"You're a mathematician?"

From her expression, Seth couldn't tell if Lauren thought that was a good or a bad thing.

The professor raised his hands and laughed. "Guilty as charged."

"Adam is back to settle his father's estate," Seth informed Lauren. "He'll be leaving soon."

It couldn't be soon enough to suit Seth.

"I'll be here awhile." Adam may have answered Seth, but he immediately focused his attention back to Lauren. "Tell me, is your father still spending holidays in Paris?"

Lauren's smile teetered and Seth saw the strain around her eyes.

Apparently Adam didn't notice because he chuckled. "Everyone in the department envied him his lifestyle."

Seth had heard enough. He knew this was a sore spot for Lauren. He wasn't about to stand here and watch Adam inadvertently pour salt in the wound. "We should get inside," he said brusquely. "Dani is getting cold."

He didn't give Adam a chance to respond. Instead, Seth lifted his daughter from the sleigh then herded Lauren and Adam to the house.

"I'm sorry to hear about your dad." Lauren waited for Adam to open the door of the two-story home. "Had he been ill long?"

"Dad had numerous health issues." The smile that had been on Adam's mouth since he'd seen Lauren slipped from his lips. "I'd been at him to sell the place and move closer to me. But he refused. He insisted on staying out here in the middle of nowhere."

By the professor's tone it was apparent his feelings about the Big Sky state hadn't changed.

"What happened?" Lauren asked softly when Adam didn't continue.

"He had a heart attack while checking cattle." Adam pushed open the door. "Since he lived alone, it took several days for his body to be discovered."

Seth followed Lauren inside, Dani in his arms. He saw no need to mention that he'd been the one who'd found Lars.

"Lars loved this land." Seth lowered Dani to a standing position on the floor. When he was sure she was steady, he unzipped her coat. "Dying on the range was how he'd have wanted to go."

"It doesn't make it any easier." Adam cleared his throat. "I keep imagining him out there alone."

A look of sympathy crossed Lauren's face. She

rested a hand on his arm. "I can't imagine how hard this must be for you."

"I try not to think about it. I just want to get this place sold so I can get back to civilization." Adam shifted his gaze to Seth. "The attorney said you might be interested in buying the land."

"Might be." Seth took Lauren's coat from her and hung it next to Dani's on the coat tree. "But this isn't the time to talk business."

"That's right, it's Christmas." Lauren removed her stocking cap and her blonde hair spilled out, tumbling to her shoulders.

Seth had to admit she made a fetching sight. Adam apparently agreed because a look of pure masculine appreciation filled his gaze.

"I'll get your daughter and Lauren settled while you tend to the sleigh." Adam may have mentioned Dani but his eyes remained firmly fixed on Lauren.

The man's arrogant manner grated on Seth. But when Adam smiled down at Dani and asked about her accident, some of his irritation eased as his little girl blossomed.

"I broke my arm and my leg and I hit my head," Dani said happily, enjoying her time in the spotlight.

"I bet it's hard for you to get around," Adam said to Dani while sharing a smile with Lauren.

"That's why Daddy wanted Miss Lauren to move in," Dani said. "So she can take care of us."

Adam straightened slowly. He turned to Lauren, his eyes wide with shock. "You live with Anderssen?"

Seth gritted his teeth. The man made it sound as if she were shacked up with a barbarian.

"Temporarily." If Lauren noticed, it didn't show in her matter-of-fact response. "Until Dani is better."

Adam opened his mouth as if to comment, but shut it without saying a word. He gestured to an arched doorway. "We'll have our coffee and dessert in there."

Seth scooped up Dani and carried her to the living room. A fire crackled in the hearth, and an open book lay on the side table. He sat Dani down on a green floral sofa that had once been Barbara Nordstrom's pride and joy. Her death in a car accident was something Lars had never gotten over.

"I'll get the coffee," Adam said. "And some plates for the pastry."

The pastry.

Seth stifled a groan. His gaze met Lauren's and just like that, he found himself drowning in their emerald depths.

"By the way…" Adam turned back on his way to the kitchen. "Where is the Kringle?"

"I left it in the sleigh." Seth yanked his attention from Lauren. "I'll get everything settled outside and bring it in with me."

"Hurry, Daddy." Dani rubbed her midsection with her left hand. "My tummy is hungry for Kringle."

"I won't be long." Seth hesitated. He needed to get the horse out of the weather and grab the pastry, but he found himself strangely reluctant to leave Lauren.

"Don't worry, Anderssen," Adam said with a wink. "I'll take good care of *both* of them."

Lauren took a sip of wine and shot a sideways glance at Seth. They'd returned from the Nordstrom ranch a little over an hour ago. While Seth put the horse and sleigh away, she'd gotten Dani ready for bed.

It had been obvious Seth had been surprised—but pleased—when he'd come in and found his daughter already in her PJs with her eyelids drooping. By the time Seth tucked her in and opened a book to read to her, the little girl was already asleep.

Normally Lauren would be ready for bed, too, but the afternoon nap she'd taken earlier had stuck with her. The way she felt right now, she could stay up all night. Thanks to Seth it had been the best Christmas she could remember. She'd been ready to head upstairs when he'd suggested a glass of wine to cap off the evening.

While he was in the kitchen uncorking a new bottle, Lauren switched off the lamps and proceeded to light candles scattered throughout the room. The glow from the flames mingled with the light emanating from the dying embers in the hearth to give the area a warm, cozy feel.

Seth walked into the room with two glasses in hand just as Lauren lit the last candle. He glanced around. His lips quirked upward. "Did I forget to pay the electric bill?"

Lauren returned his smile and dropped back on the sofa, folding one leg beneath her. She held out a hand, feeling lighthearted and flirtatious. "Give me my glass of wine and shut up."

He handed her the goblet and took a seat on the other end of the sofa. "Dani isn't allowed to say 'shut up.'"

Lauren leaned back in the overstuffed sofa and shifted in her seat, gazing at Seth through lowered lashes. "In case you haven't noticed, I'm not Dani."

"Oh, I've noticed." Seth's blue eyes glittered in the dim light.

Her heart pounded a provocative Latin beat against her ribs. Still, Lauren kept a tight hold on her rising excitement as she traced the rim of her glass with one finger. "You want to hear something funny?"

Seth smiled encouragingly.

The darkness surrounding them made it easy for her to speak freely. "When you were in the stable, Adam asked if we were dating."

Lauren hadn't been surprised by the question. Only that he hadn't asked sooner. She'd sensed Adam's interest from the moment he'd discovered she was related to his mentor.

"I wonder what gave him that impression?"

Lauren lifted a shoulder in a slight shrug. "When Dani mentioned we'll all be living under the same roof, I'm sure that made him curious about our relationship."

Though that was the obvious answer, Lauren had a feeling Adam had picked up on the sexual tension between her and Seth. Every time Seth's hand brushed her, every time he sent a smile her way, she'd turned into a blithering idiot. When he'd sat beside her on the sofa in the Nordstrom living room, she'd had difficulty concentrating on the conversation. They'd been thigh-to-thigh, arm-to-arm, and all she could think was how good it would feel if there were no clothes between them.

"I'm sure Adam understands that you're simply Dani's nanny," Seth said. "Not my girlfriend or my—" his voice faltered, and he took a gulp of wine "—lover."

"You're right," Lauren said. "Just because we'll be living under the same roof doesn't automatically make us lovers."

Lauren rather liked the way the word rolled off her tongue. It conjured up visions of muscular arms holding her close, calloused cowboy hands caressing her bare skin and warm lips covering hers. The vivid image brought with it an ache of wanting.

From the way Seth's eyes darkened, he appeared to be doing some visualizing—and aching—of his own.

The realization buoyed her flagging spirits. A couple times at the Nordstrom ranch, she'd gotten the feeling Seth was trying to foist her off on Adam. It was confusing considering the pull between them. Still the feeling persisted.

"I was surprised he had to ask," Lauren said. "Considering your behavior."

"What about my behavior?"

She had to chuckle. "You were like a yenta determined to make a match."

Seth's brows pulled together, his expression clearly puzzled. "Beg pardon?"

Lauren swirled the wine in her glass. "You played up the fact that Adam and I are both academicians. You told him I was a big-city girl at least three times."

He grimaced. "Did I really?"

Lauren nodded.

"You're right. He probably didn't know what to think." Seth's gaze searched hers. "Did he ask you out?"

"Not yet."

"Think he will?"

"Probably." Actually, there was no doubt in her mind. The way he'd looked at her, coupled with his question about her relationship with Seth, told her the mathematician would be picking up the phone.

"Will you go?"

"I doubt it," Lauren answered honestly. Though Adam seemed to be a nice-enough guy, he reminded her too much of her father. But she didn't tell Seth that part. "Between finishing up my dissertation, meeting with clients and taking care of Dani, I won't have much free time. I'd rather spend what time I do have with Anna or Stacie."

"Do you ever feel the need for male-female interaction?" he asked.

Lauren straightened in her seat. Her heart, which had finally settled back into a nice easy rhythm, sped up. Was he asking the question on behalf of Adam? Or himself? Had he felt the pull between them but wasn't going to act on it until he knew where she stood?

She had two options—play coy or be honest.

She'd never been good at playing games.

"I miss sex," Lauren admitted, staring into the burgundy liquid. "While I may not have time to date, I could be persuaded to fit a purely physical affair into my schedule."

Lauren looked up at the strangled sound coming from Seth's throat. She lifted a brow. "You okay?"

"Are you saying you'd be interested in a relationship based solely on sex?"

"That's the only kind I've ever known," Lauren confessed. The confines of the darkened room allowed her to speak honestly.

"Ever?"

"Ever."

"How many of these relationships have you had?" Curiosity, rather than judgment, underscored the question.

"Not many." Lauren hated to admit how few. For a thirty-one-year-old modern female, her experience was extremely limited.

"How did you meet these guys?"

"I met Ruis at a symposium on global warming. There was an instant spark between us." Lauren's lips lifted in a slight smile, remembering the passionate Spaniard. "I was twenty-two at the time. I'd never had a boyfriend before him. We became intimate almost immediately. I thought he was in love with me. But after a while he made me see that the great fire between us existed only in bed. I should have known. After all, we were very different people. But on the positive side, Ruis taught me a relationship based on sex could be workable."

Seth muttered something she couldn't understand then met her gaze. "What about the others?"

"There was only one other." Lauren twisted the stem of her wineglass between her fingers. "About five years ago."

"How did you meet him?"

"His father taught at the community college with me. Dirk worked on oil rigs in the Gulf. We both loved to hike and ski. But he'd be out on a platform for six months at a time so whenever he came home he had a lot of pent-up passion. Sometimes we'd go to the mountains but most of the time…we didn't."

Seth's gaze narrowed.

"That worked fine for me," Lauren hastened to add. "Because I was busy, too."

Seth met her gaze. "You deserve better than you got from either of those men."

"Like I said." Lauren tried to smile but her lips were stiff and refused to move. "It worked out for everyone."

"If you say so."

A cold feeling of dread coursed through Lauren's veins. She shifted uneasily in her seat. Her two best friends had never understood her past relationships. What had made her think Seth would?

Because he's alone, a tiny voice whispered. Because his needs aren't being met. Because you thought he wanted you in that way, too.

"Forget what I said." Lauren brushed her hair back from her face with a hand that trembled slightly. "I thought you'd understand."

Seth's gaze turned curious.

"Anna told me you promised Jan you wouldn't marry until Dani is out of high school."

"It's a promise I intend to keep."

"Physically it has to be hard," Lauren said carefully. "Especially when you have options."

"I won't lead a woman on just so I can sleep with her." A muscle in his jaw jumped. "That's not me."

"I realize you're not that kind of man," Lauren agreed. "But there's another alternative."

Seth raised a brow.

"Find a woman who can be content with no-strings-attached sex."

"Someone like you?" he asked in a low voice, the dim light blanketing his face in shadows.

She couldn't see his eyes, but the electricity was back, stronger than ever, sizzling and popping.

"Yes." Lauren took a breath and plunged ahead. "Someone like me."

Chapter Seven

Seth thanked God he was sitting because otherwise the wave of longing that washed over him would have knocked him off his feet. Having such a lovely woman offer to have no-strings-attached sex was a beautiful dream. And his worst nightmare. Because no matter how much—physically—he wanted to say yes, what she was suggesting was not an option.

"I'm flattered." Seth gentled his tone and chose his next words carefully. "You're a beautiful woman, both inside and out. And there's this chemistry between us that I can't explain, but…"

"But?" The smile on Lauren's lips froze.

"I can't do it."

"I don't understand the problem." Even as she pressed the issue, her voice turned cool, almost detached. The expression on her face gave nothing away.

"The problem is me." Seth placed his glass on the end table but kept his hands at his sides, resisting the urge to touch her. "I'm a father, a role model for my daughter. I want her to grow up believing that making love is something special that happens between a man and a woman who love each other, who've made a commitment to each other."

"I wasn't suggesting that Dani be informed we were having sex," Lauren said stiffly.

"I know you weren't," Seth said. "But kids seem to have an uncanny way of finding out things. And even if she didn't, I would know I wasn't practicing what I'll soon be preaching to her."

Lauren lifted the wineglass to her lips and took a big gulp. "You're right," she said. "Forget I mentioned it."

Damn it all to hell. He'd hurt her. Just what he'd sworn not to do.

"Thank you for the offer, though." Impulsively Seth reached over and took her hand. Despite the proximity to the fire, her fingers were ice cold.

He thought she might pull away, but once again she surprised him. For a long moment he sat there with his fingers entwined with hers in silent companionship. Seth wanted to tell her *this* was what he'd really missed. He missed sitting in front of the fire and talking about his day. He missed hearing about someone else's day. He missed the closeness.

And, if he was being completely honest, he'd admit he missed the sex, as well. He was a man, after all. There was nothing like being pleasured and bringing pleasure to someone you loved. It was the desire for such intimacy that made him drop her hand.

Despite knowing and believing that everything he'd said to her was one hundred percent true, at the moment he wasn't feeling particularly strong. The stirrings in his body told him he needed to back off and put some distance between them.

He stood. "I should call it a night."

"Yes, let's both call it a night." Lauren jumped to her feet. "Morning will be here before we know it."

She started toward the stairs, then stopped and turned, a swath of the most becoming shade of pink emerging across her cheeks. "I want you to know that this was the most wonderful Christmas I've ever had."

"For me, too," he said softly as she started up the stairs. "For me, too."

If she heard him, she gave no sign. Instead she continued to climb the stairs with methodical precision as she headed to her room alone.

Watching her go, he figured he deserved a medal...for either being a responsible parent or the biggest fool on the planet.

Lauren stared at the overnight bag. When she'd unpacked it yesterday, she'd been filled with excitement. The holidays had been something to look forward to with anticipation rather than dread.

She zipped the bag shut and sat on the bed next to it. Sunlight streamed through the window but the warmth brought no comfort.

Regret oozed from every pore in her body. In the clear light of day, it was easy to see how she'd let the holiday spirit cloud her thinking. Unfortunately she couldn't take back the words. Dear God, what must Seth think of her now? She'd practically spread her legs and said, "Here I am, take me."

She chuckled at the image. Okay, so maybe it hadn't been quite that bad, but it had been awkward. And she didn't see how she could be Dani's nanny. Not now. Every time she looked at Seth, or touched his hand, he'd be thinking she wanted to jump him. But that wouldn't be the worst of it. Last night, for the briefest of moments, she'd seen pity reflected in his blue eyes.

He hadn't understood her relationships with Ruis and Dirk. Granted, most times a purely sexual relationship ended up hurting one of the parties involved. But that hadn't happened in her case. She'd been as satisfied as the men. Still, she could see where that might be a hard concept for a Montana cowboy to wrap his head around.

A knock at her bedroom door yanked Lauren from her reverie and jerked her to standing.

"Lauren. It's me, Anna. Can I come in?"

Lauren exhaled a relieved breath. For a second she'd thought it was Seth. Eventually they'd have to talk about last night. But at least with his sister here, it wouldn't be before she'd had her coffee.

"Lauren? Are you there?"

"Since when do you need permission to come into my bedroom?" Lauren pulled the door open, her spirits lifting at the sight of her friend.

As always, Anna looked like a model. From the heels of her cocoa-colored leather boots to her tweed skirt with a wide belt cinching her sweater close, the look was both fashionable and flattering. Even her honey-colored hair was artfully messy.

But it was her dazzling smile that Lauren noticed. Since reuniting with Mitch, Anna wore her happiness on her sleeve. It surrounded her and bathed everyone near in its glow. Lauren fought back a pang of envy. What would it be like to be so much in love…and to be loved so much in return?

"Merry day-after-Christmas." Anna pulled her close in an exuberant hug. "I wanted so much to be here yesterday."

"I heard Mitch got stuck."

"He was a bit frustrated." Anna released Lauren and stepped back, her eyes twinkling. "You can't believe how much snow we got. It was like the sky opened up and dumped a ton of the white stuff right over our house."

"Well, you were both missed," Lauren said.

"That's sweet but I'm sure you did fine without me." Anna gazed at Lauren through lowered lashes. "Seth told me you guys had a fabulous time. I want to hear all about it."

Seth had told his sister he'd had a *fabulous* time? What else had he told her?

"Where is your brother?" Lauren asked, stalling for time.

"Ooh, I'm glad you asked." Anna grabbed Lauren's hand and pulled her into the hall. "He and Mitch went out to the stable to check on some horse that's sick. I promised we'd make breakfast before they take us into town."

By now Lauren's head was spinning. "Why into town? And where is Dani?"

"She's downstairs coloring and *very* excited about you

being her nanny," Anna said. "She couldn't stop talking about you. You've made quite an impression on my niece."

"Dani is the sweetest little girl." Lauren swallowed past the sudden lump in her throat. Who would Seth get to watch her now? Lauren told herself it was none of her concern, yet she couldn't help worrying.

"Let's go see the little princess." Anna turned and started down the stairs. "And get that breakfast started."

Lauren had to practically run to catch up to her. "What's the hurry?"

"As soon as we eat, I need to scoot. I promised Cassie I'd help man the shop for the after-Christmas sale." Anna tossed the words over her shoulder, the fondness for her new partner evident in her tone.

"I didn't know you were having a sale."

"It was Cassie's idea," Anna said. "I'm not sure how much business we'll have but it's worth a shot."

"I get to go to the shop with Aunt Anna," Dani called from the kitchen, apparently hearing their voices. "She's going to put me to work."

Lauren followed Anna into the room, realizing she'd have to wait a little longer to tell her about the change in the nanny plans.

"What are you going to do for your aunt?" Lauren asked, moving to the counter to start the coffee. It was crazy, but after one day she already felt comfortable in Seth's kitchen.

"Something with squares." Dani sat at the table hunched over the coloring book she'd gotten for Christmas, looking absolutely adorable in a fuzzy pink sweater. "Right, Aunt Anna?"

"That's correct, sweetheart." Anna dropped a kiss on her niece's head before pulling a frying pan from the drawer beneath the oven. "She's going to organize quilt squares for me."

While Anna rattled on about the shop and put long strips of bacon in the skillet, Lauren got the coffee brewing.

"You're in for a special treat this morning." Anna cracked a couple of eggs into a mixing bowl. "I'm going to whip up my secret French toast mixture."

"I think your secret ingredient is nothing more than vanilla," Lauren teased her friend.

"I think—" Anna laughed "—that you should mind your own business and shut up."

"Daddy won't like that," Dani said loudly. "You shouldn't say 'shut up.'"

"That's right, princess."

Lauren's heart skipped a beat. With her back to the door, she hadn't noticed Seth's arrival. Taking a deep breath, she turned. "Breakfast should be ready in just a few minutes. If you want to wash up—"

"First I need to know something." Seth hooked his thumbs into his belt loops and rocked back on his heels.

Dear God, surely he wasn't going to bring up anything about last night in front of Anna or Dani.

"Which one of you said 'shut up'?" Seth asked.

Lauren released the breath she hadn't realized she'd been holding.

Anna raised her hand. "Guilty. But only because Lauren was giving away my secret ingredient."

"Still, 'shut up' is never appropriate." A smile tugged at the corners of Seth's lips.

"You can say whatever you want." Mitch walked into the kitchen, flecks of snow on his dark hair. "Don't let your brother push you around."

"But she was telling Miss Lauren to shut up, Uncle Mitch," Dani said, looking up from her coloring book.

"Is that true?" Mitch asked, looking even more amused than Seth.

Anna lifted her shoulders in a shrug, her blue eyes twinkling.

"I like it when your aunt Anna tells me to shut up." Mitch moved to his wife's side and slipped his arms around her waist. "Especially when she says 'shut up and kiss me, cowboy.'"

Anna wrapped her arms around Mitch's neck and wove her fingers through his hair. "Shut up and kiss me, cowboy."

The words had barely left Anna's mouth when Mitch's lips closed over hers.

The emotion and passion between the two was so powerful that Lauren had to look away. She busied herself turning on the electric griddle and dipping the bread into Anna's secret recipe. She'd barely dropped the first slices on the hot flat surface when Dani's giggle split the air.

"That's just how Santa kissed Miss Lauren," Dani said, her voice filled with triumph.

Lauren winced, closing her eyes for a second, then resumed dipping the bread into the batter and putting the slices on the griddle.

Out of the corner of her eye she saw Anna turn in her husband's arms. "What?"

"I was supposed to be asleep." Dani's little voice

trembled with excitement. "When I heard the bells, I knew it was Santa Claus. I got out of bed and moved real quiet to the door. That's when I saw Santa kissing Miss Lauren."

"Wow." Anna shot a sideways glance at her brother. "That must have been really exciting."

Lauren turned, spatula in hand. "The French toast is almost done. Would someone like to set the table?"

"I'll do it." Anna brushed another kiss across her husband's lips before opening the silverware drawer. "But let's talk a bit more about your romantic interlude with, ah, Santa?"

"I don't think this is an appropriate discussion—"

"Save your breath, Seth," Anna said. "You're just upset 'cause you weren't there. You weren't there, right?"

If looks could kill, Anna Donavan would be dead.

"I was upstairs." Seth's blue eyes flashed a warning his sister seemed determined to ignore.

"Upstairs?" Anna said. "How convenient."

Dani tilted her head, her brow furrowed. "What's 'convenient'?"

Seth shot Mitch a look that practically begged for assistance but his brother-in-law simply grinned.

"I just meant it's too bad your dad missed Santa," Anna said.

Lauren swallowed a groan when Anna's gaze returned to her. "Tell us, Lauren. Was Santa a good kisser?"

Growing up, Lauren had always wanted a sister. But seeing the pleasure Anna was getting from tormenting her brother, Lauren could now clearly see the downside of sibling love.

"He was…okay," Lauren said.

"I think she liked him," Dani said to her aunt. "She was hugging him really, really tight."

"Interesting." Anna placed the plates on the table, barely able to contain her smile. "You'll have to remember to tell me more about this experience, Lauren."

Lauren sighed. "Somehow I don't think you'll let me forget."

Anna laughed. "You've got that right, girlfriend. You've definitely got that right."

Chapter Eight

Sew-fisticated, the small shop that Anna co-owned with former classmate Cassie Els, buzzed with activity. Dani, along with Cassie's youngest boy, Brandon, sat in the back sorting fabric squares while Lauren helped Cassie and Anna man the cash registers. Trenton, Cassie's oldest, had planned to watch the younger kids, but the twelve-year-old had gotten sick during the night and was home in bed.

Thankfully, Dani and Brandon hadn't been very demanding, because the traffic in the store had been incredible. In only a few short weeks the shop had become the unofficial gathering place for women in the community. Though there was more talking than selling going on, the upcoming quilting and scrapbooking classes, which had been half-filled before Christmas, were now full.

Lauren had been waiting all morning for Anna to take a break. She wanted to talk to her privately before Mitch and Seth returned.

Once they got past the kiss, and she confessed to propositioning her best friend's brother, she hoped Anna would understand why she had to back out of her agreement with Seth.

"Would you mind running over to the Coffee Pot and picking up another pot of apple cider?" Cassie asked, her cheeks flushed with happiness. "I think one more should be plenty."

"I'd be happy to." Lauren started toward the door, then stopped. "What about Dani?"

Cassie glanced toward the back room. "I'll keep an eye on her. And Anna will be here, too."

Lauren caught Anna's eye. Her friend stopped talking, er, selling, just long enough to offer a little wave. Lauren could only hope Seth wouldn't get back early, so she and Anna would have time to talk.

After dropping "the girls" off at the shop, Seth and Mitch had left to do some handyman work at the home of one of the town's senior citizens. Apparently doing such good deeds the day after Christmas was a tradition for the men of Sweet River.

Lauren pulled her jacket off the hook. As she wrapped the thin fabric around her, her thoughts drifted back to yesterday. She remembered how Seth had insisted she take his coat so she wouldn't get cold. He'd been such a gentleman.

Her lips twisted in a wry smile. She should have

known better than to think he'd be interested in a fling. But she was through beating herself up over the error in judgment. She pushed open the door and practically stumbled over Loretta Barbee, the pastor's wife.

"Mrs. Barbee. Merry Christmas." Lauren tried to step around her but Loretta shifted to block her way. NFL linebackers had nothing on this woman.

"We missed you at church yesterday."

"The weather was turning bad," Lauren found herself explaining. "Seth didn't want to take the chance on getting stuck in town."

"That explains why Seth Anderssen wasn't there." Loretta's eyes narrowed. "That doesn't explain *your* absence from God's house."

"But I was with Seth." The words popped out before Lauren could stop them.

The woman's hand rose to her chest. Her beady eyes widened. "You spent the night?"

"I spent Christmas with Seth and Dani." Lauren lifted her chin. "In the guest bedroom."

Though she'd answered factually, Lauren immediately regretted the abruptness of her response.

"Tsk-tsk. No need to be so defensive," the older woman chided. "I was merely making conversation."

"I'm sorry." Lauren offered the woman a conciliatory smile. "It's been a long day. I just meant—"

"No need to explain, dear. I can see you're in a hurry. I'll let you get on your way. Have a nice day." The minister's wife turned abruptly and opened the door to Anna's shop.

It took until Lauren reached the Coffee Pot for her embarrassment to ease. She stood for a moment and breathed in the enticing aromas of Stacie's culinary creations before stepping inside.

The bells over the door heralded her arrival. Norm and Al, two café regulars, glanced up from their game of checkers. Lauren returned their smiles, then glanced around the dining area, impressed at how the changes Stacie had made in the past few months were coming together.

The first to go had been the teapot-and-flower wallpaper. It had been replaced with caramel-colored paint. Then Josh had ripped the knotty pine paneling off a far wall and left the brick exposed. The wagon-wheel light fixtures were trashed soon after, energy-efficient ceiling fans taking their place. Still, despite the alterations, the café retained its small-town charm.

Business had soared since Stacie had started doing most of the cooking. But today, other than the two checkers players, the place was deserted.

Stacie's laughter sounded from the kitchen seconds before the swinging door opened. The newlywed swept into the room, dressed in coat and mittens, her arms filled with two big boxes. Her face brightened when she saw her friend. "Happy day-after-Christmas, Lauren."

"Same to you." Lauren hurried and took the top box from Stacie's arms. It was heavier than she'd expected. "What do you have in here? Bricks?"

"Just food for the shelter." Stacie paused. "I'm making a delivery. Care to join me? It'll give us a chance to catch up, and I sure could use an extra pair of hands."

Lauren hesitated. "Anna sent me to pick up more apple cider for the Sew-fisticated open house."

"The church where the shelter is housed is only a

couple blocks away, so the delivery shouldn't take long." Stacie's tone turned persuasive. "If you help me out, I'll not only get that cider for you, I'll throw in a little something extra."

Lauren thought quickly. From what she'd observed, the Sew-fisticated customers were doing more talking than drinking. With hot coffee and tea available, they probably wouldn't miss the cider…at least not for the next half hour. "I'd love to take a walk in the crisp Montana air with you."

"Uh-oh, sounds like it hasn't warmed up much."

"It's not too bad." Lauren settled her gaze on Stacie's fur-trimmed parka. "You won't be cold. Not in that coat."

"What about you?" Stacie's brow furrowed. "Yours doesn't look very warm."

"I'll be fine." Lauren waved a dismissive hand. "I can't wait to hear all about your Christmas with Josh. Was it as wonderful as you'd hoped?"

"It was fabulous." Stacie's face glowed, just as Anna's did when she talked about *her* new husband. "Josh made it special for me."

"I'm sure you made it special for him, too." Lauren realized with a sudden start that she didn't envy Stacie her "fabulous" Christmas. Not one bit.

Probably because you had your own memorable holiday with Seth and Dani.

Al jumped up from his checkerboard to open the door, and as they ambled down the sidewalk, Stacie recounted every last detail of her Christmas, including the sumptuous meal she and Josh had made for his mom and dad.

"They'd barely left when my family called," Stacie continued. "I was able to speak with my brother and sisters and all my nieces and nephews. And my parents, of course. Did I tell you they're planning to come here next Christmas?"

"That's great news, Stacie." Lauren tried to summon up some enthusiasm, but all she could think was that *her* parents hadn't even bothered to call this year.

As if she could read Lauren's thoughts, Stacie turned, her eyes dark with sympathy. "By the look on your face, I take it you didn't hear from Edmund and Margaret."

"Not a peep." Lauren tightened her gloved hands around the box. "They were probably having so much fun in Paris that I didn't even cross their minds."

"That must hurt," Stacie said.

The caring in her friend's voice brought a lump to Lauren's throat. She shrugged and continued walking.

"Forget the parents. We have more important things to discuss." Stacie shot Lauren a sly glance. "Like you and Seth."

Heat rose up Lauren's neck. Rather than meet Stacie's assessing gaze, she focused on the church, now only a half block ahead. "I had a pleasant Christmas with Seth and Dani, if that's what you're asking."

"*Hot* Christmas, more like." Stacie laughed aloud. "Anna told me about the kiss."

Lauren accepted that news traveled quickly in a small town, but Anna had been with her most of the day. "How did you hear? *When* did you hear?"

"Blame it on the wonders of modern technology." Stacie chuckled and hopped forward to avoid an errant snowball thrown from a side street. "Anna called me from her cell on her way into town. But I need details. The only thing specific I got from Anna was that Seth was wearing a Santa suit."

Lauren smiled, remembering the softness of the red velour and the intoxicating taste of Seth's warm, sweet lips. "There's something about a man in a Santa suit that is incredibly appealing."

"I agree." Stacie sighed. "The only thing that trumps a man in uniform for sexiness is a cowboy wearing nothing but a Stetson."

"I wouldn't know about that." Lauren ignored the twinkle in her friend's eyes and kept her tone offhand. "We didn't get naked. We only kissed."

"Bet you liked it, though."

"The kiss?" Lauren's heart picked up speed. "It was okay."

"Methinks it was more than okay."

"You're right," Lauren admitted, knowing Stacie wouldn't give up until she told the truth. "On a scale of one to ten, I'd give it a twenty."

"Wow. Super hot. It really didn't go further?" Stacie paused and slanted a sideways glance at Lauren.

Lauren shook her head. "Dani came out of her bedroom and saw me kissing Santa—er, Seth."

"It's like something out of a movie." Stacie's eyes turned dreamy. "Wouldn't it be fabulous if you and Seth fell in love, got married, settled in Sweet—"

"Stop right there," Lauren said, finding the scenario way too appealing. "My plans don't include Sweet River *or* handsome cowboys."

"So you think Seth is handsome."

Lauren let a groan be her answer.

"I had plans, remember?" Stacie's expression was suddenly serious. "But I figured out a way I could have Josh and my dreams, too."

"It worked for you," Lauren admitted. "And I'm happy it did. But there is no way—"

"Where there's a will, there's *always* a way," Stacie said, punctuating the cliché with a decisive nod.

"I'll keep that in mind," Lauren said with a wry smile, climbing the steps of the church, then repositioning the box in her hands so she could open the door.

When Lauren had first heard Sweet River had a homeless shelter, she'd been surprised. She hadn't thought there would be much of a need in the area. But the cots set up in several Sunday-school classrooms and the fifteen or so people waiting for food in the church's makeshift dining hall challenged that assumption.

Stacie stopped to speak with the minister about an upcoming fund-raiser and Lauren began unpacking the food. She'd started on the second box when Stacie touched her shoulder.

"A volunteer who was supposed to help serve didn't show," Stacie said in a low tone. "I'm going to stay for a bit. Shirley should be able to handle the café alone for the next hour or so."

"I can stay and help, too," Lauren said.

"That's sweet of you to offer, but they only need one more body, and you should get back to Anna and the shop," Stacie said. "If you'd just tell Shirley I'll be back in time for the supper rush, I'd appreciate it."

"Consider it done," Lauren said.

"And tell her to give you a couple dozen sugar cookies to go with that cider," Stacie added before turning her attention back to the minister.

Lauren visited with a couple of the shelter residents for several minutes, then strolled back to the café, enjoying the sound of the snow crunching beneath her feet.

Her destination was in sight when a fire truck shot down Main Street, sirens screaming. The door to the community center burst open as a second truck zoomed by. Lauren jumped back as a bunch of cowboys spilled out onto the sidewalk and scattered.

"What's going on?" she called out to one of Seth's friends as he raced by.

"Fire on Elmwood," Wes Danker yelled without breaking stride.

A chill traveled up Lauren's spine. If she wasn't mistaken, Elmwood was the next street over from where Mitch and Seth were working. Instead of entering the café, Lauren wrapped her coat more tightly around her and watched each man pile into his truck, put a flashing light on the dash and take off down the street.

When they'd first moved to Sweet River, Anna had mentioned that the town was too small to have professional firefighters. Instead, it depended on trained volunteers. And hadn't she also said *Seth* was one of those volunteers?

The apple cider forgotten, Lauren turned and ran down the street to Sew-fisticated. Though she hadn't been gone all that long, the shop was deserted. Cassie was nowhere to be seen. Anna was missing, too. In fact, the front part of the store was empty save for Marg Millstead, Mitch's stepmother, manning the cash register.

"Where's Anna?" Lauren asked, her breath coming in short puffs. "And Cassie?"

"They had to run an errand," Dani called out from the back room.

"They took my mom's car," Brandon added.

Marg put a finger to her lips. She grabbed Lauren's arm and propelled her to the very front of the store, far from little ears. "We need to talk."

Lauren's heart skipped a beat at the worry furrowing the older woman's brow. "Tell me."

"There was a fire at the house Cassie rents." Marg spoke in a whisper. "The sheriff called not long after you left. Apparently Seth and Mitch were the first to respond. They thought the house was empty, but—"

"Trenton was upstairs." The words spilled from Lauren's lips as she remembered what Cassie had said earlier. "He hadn't been feeling well and stayed home in bed."

"When Seth and Mitch heard him calling for help, they went in without waiting for backup." Marg paused and drew a shuddering breath. "Trenton and Mitch got out just as part of the roof collapsed. They were very lucky."

"What about Seth?" Lauren's entire body turned to ice. Her heart beat so hard and fast, the room began to spin.

"Seth was trapped by the falling debris."

Lauren covered her mouth. Only the knowledge that she needed to stay strong for the little girl in the other room kept her from crying out.

"Mitch went back for Seth," Marg continued. "By that time Josh had arrived. Together they got him out."

Lowering her hand, Lauren exhaled a ragged breath. Perhaps it wasn't as bad as she'd feared. "So Trenton is okay?"

Marg nodded. "He was very lucky."

"And Seth?" Lauren asked. "Is he okay, too?"

The older woman hesitated. "They think so."

"What do you mean, *they think so?*" Lauren's voice started to rise, but she immediately pulled it back down.

"The ambulance is taking him to the medical center in Big Timber." Marg's eyes filled with tears. "They're concerned about how much smoke he inhaled."

Lauren didn't realize her own tears were falling until she felt the wetness against her cheeks. "I need to go to him."

Marg grabbed Lauren's arm before she reached the door. "Anna called. She's in the ambulance with her brother. Mitch is following behind in the truck. She wants you to take care of Dani. She'll call as soon as she knows anything."

Though she knew Marg hadn't meant to be unkind, Lauren felt as if she'd been put in her place. There was no reason for her to rush to Seth's side. He had his family with him. She was just his daughter's nanny.

Dani.

"Does Dani know about her dad?"

Marg shook her head.

"I think Anna hoped you'd tell her." There was an appealing look in the woman's eyes. "What with you being into counseling and all."

Lauren closed her eyes for a second. To be an effective therapist you needed to be detached. Right now she didn't feel very detached. In fact, she felt way too connected. But who else was there? And it had to be done with great sensitivity.

"I'll do it." Lauren drew a steadying breath. "What about Brandon? Should I take him with me, too?"

"Not necessary," Marg said. "Alex Darst is on his way to pick up the boy."

Only then did Lauren remember that Cassie and Alex were dating. "I wonder where they're going to sleep tonight? Certainly not at Alex's place. His apartment is teeny-tiny."

It was ridiculous to be standing here discussing housing options. But anything was better than thinking about Seth in that ambulance.

"I'll give Cassie some options." The sympathetic look in Marg's eyes said she understood Lauren's need to focus on something besides Seth. "Are you taking Dani to your house?"

"For now," Lauren said then stopped. "I don't have a way to get there. Seth was going to pick us up after he finished…"

Lauren blinked rapidly. She would not cry.

"Henry is bringing over Seth's truck," Marg said. "He can drive you and Dani if you'd like."

"I'll be fine…."

"At least let him help you get her into the truck." Marg's hand squeezed Lauren's shoulder in gentle comfort.

"Miss Lauren, I'm getting hungry," Dani called out. "When are we going to go home?"

"In a little bit." Lauren was thankful her voice gave nothing away. "First we're going to stop by my house."

Dani chattered nonstop on the short drive. Lauren let her talk, murmuring an encouraging word every now and then.

The large two-story where they were headed had originally belonged to Anna's great-grandmother. She'd inherited it several years ago when her grandma Borghild had died.

Dani pressed her face against the passenger's-side window when they pulled into the drive. "I can't wait to tell Daddy about everything I did today."

Lauren slowed the truck to a stop and shut off the ignition. In the course of her studies and in her counseling sessions, she'd had to discuss many difficult topics, but none more difficult than this. Dani had already lost one parent. How would she cope if anything happened to her dad?

Think positive.

Lauren took a deep steadying breath and turned in the seat to face the child. "Your daddy did something really brave this afternoon."

Dani's sweet little face brightened. "He did?"

"Yes, he did." Lauren forced a smile. "There was a fire at Brandon's house. Your dad and your uncle Mitch went in and helped Brandon's brother, Trenton, get out of the house safely."

"Daddy does that a lot," Dani said. "He likes to help people."

"I know he does." Lauren dug her fingernails into her palms.

"When he comes home for dinner, I'm going to give

him a big hug," Dani said, a smile lifting her lips. "He likes my hugs."

Lauren took a breath. And then another. "The thing is…I'm not sure your daddy will be home for dinner."

Dani's blond brows pulled together. "Why not?"

"Well, you know how when fire burns, there's a lot of smoke?"

Dani slowly nodded.

"Your daddy breathed in some of that smoke. Before he comes home, he has to get his lungs checked out at the hospital."

Though Lauren tried to keep all emotion from her voice, she must not have been successful because the child's big blue eyes filled with tears.

"I'm sure he'll be fine," Lauren hastened to add. "Aunt Anna and Uncle Mitch are with him and they're going to call and let us know when he'll be coming home."

"I want my daddy." Tears slipped down the child's face. "I want to talk to my daddy."

Lauren leaned forward and unbuckled Dani from her safety belt. She wrapped the child in her arms, holding her as close as the casts would allow. Still, Dani continued to cry, deep shuddering sobs that racked her body. It seemed she would never stop, but finally, sniffles and ragged breaths replaced the sobs.

Lauren grabbed a tissue from her purse and handed it to the girl. "I'm going to call Aunt Anna and see if you can talk to your daddy. Okay?"

"'Kay." Dani hiccuped and swiped at her nose.

But before Lauren could dial Anna's cell, the phone rang.

"Lauren?" The voice was hoarse and rough as sand-paper, but she recognized it immediately.

"Seth." Joy sluiced through Lauren's veins. She tightened her fingers around the phone. "Thank God."

"Is Dani with you?"

"She is, and she wants to talk to you," Lauren said. "Are you okay?"

A fit of coughing was the only answer for a long moment. "Sorry 'bout that. Yeah, I'm going to be fine. Look, would it be possible for you to begin watching Dani right away? I know you weren't planning to start until after the first, but it will be a while before I'm at full speed."

By the time he finished the request, his voice was so faint she could barely hear him and the coughing had started up again.

"I want to talk to Daddy," Dani demanded, reaching for the phone.

Lauren lifted a finger and shook her head. "Just a second," she mouthed to the girl.

"Of course," Lauren said to Seth. "I'll take her home in a little bit and bring my stuff with me."

"I owe you," Seth said, the relief in his voice evident.

"No worries," Lauren said. "You can count on me."

And, as she handed the phone to Dani, she realized it was true. He could count on her.

Last night had been a mere blip on the radar. Tonight they would start over.

Chapter Nine

"It's ten feet to the front door," Seth said to his friends when the truck stopped in front of his house. "I can make it on my own."

His bravado must have convinced Josh and Mitch, because they relaxed their grip on the door handle. He'd insisted he didn't need their help to get from the hospital to the truck, but thankfully they'd ignored his protests. It was nearly impossible for him to take a deep breath. And any exertion seemed to set off a spell of coughing that left his legs weak and shaky.

The doctor in Big Timber had sent him home with an inhaler and told him to take next week off. He had a follow-up appointment in ten days. Hopefully he'd be ready to resume his ranch duties at that time. His foreman would have to pick up the slack until then.

Seth's hand closed over the door handle but instead of opening it, he paused for a moment calling on his inner reserve. It was important to him that Dani not worry. Once he got to the front door, he wanted everything to appear as normal as possible. That's why his sister wasn't here. And why Josh and Mitch weren't coming in.

"We don't mind hanging around for a while to make sure you're okay," Mitch said, two lines of worry etched between his brow.

"Yeah, you're not lookin' so good," Josh observed.

"I appreciate everything you've done." Seth's voice shook with pent-up emotion. He owed these guys a debt he'd never be able to repay. Thanks to their courage, his daughter still had a father. And he still had a life. "I'll be fine. Lauren is here to take care of Dani—"

"But what about you?" Josh's tone may have been nonchalant but the concern in his eyes gave him away. "Doc Mason said—"

"I'll be fine," Seth repeated, more firmly this time.

Out of the corner of his eye, Seth saw Mitch tilt his head, his gaze sharp and assessing.

"I can't believe we didn't see it." Mitch shook his head. "All the way out here you've been trying to tell us but we haven't been listening."

"Tell us what?" Josh said.

"Lauren is inside. Seth here is eager to soak up some of her TLC." Mitch's grin widened. "He doesn't want us around 'cause we'll cramp his style."

"You and Lauren?" Josh whistled. "You've been holding out on us."

Seth shot Mitch a sharp glance. "It's not like that—"

"Dani already caught 'em smoochin'," Mitch continued. "When he was wearing a Santa suit, no less."

"Women love men in uniform. It's a big turn-on." Josh rubbed his chin. "I'd like to borrow that suit sometime. Stacie'd get a kick out of it."

Seth held on to his temper with both hands. He knew they were just trying to distract him…as well as have a little fun at his expense. They didn't realize Lauren was off-limits. The last thing he wanted was for his friends to have the wrong impression. But he was tired of listening, tired of talking, tired of explaining. He had more important things on his mind…like seeing his little girl.

He pushed open the door, but before he stepped outside, Seth turned back to his friends. "I'll give you a call in a day or two and let you know how I'm doing."

"You're not getting rid of us that easily," Mitch said.

"We'll be back tomorrow to help out." Josh met Seth's gaze. "Swen knows to call us if he needs anything before then."

Seth thought about telling them his foreman could handle anything that came up but he saved his breath. Josh and Mitch wouldn't listen anyway. Even though they'd done so much already, they were determined to help some more. "The only thing I need is for you two to get home to your wives."

Before they could protest, he stepped from the truck and headed straight for the house. By the time he reached the foyer, he was out of breath. He leaned back against the door, cursing the weakness that left him as unsteady as a newborn calf. He hoped Dani wasn't too upset or worried. Or, if she was, that he would be able to find the right words to make her feel better.

Sloughing off his coat, Seth stood for a moment in the entryway, gathering his strength, drinking in all that was familiar. The ticking of the mantel clock in the living room. Dani's giggles coming from the kitchen. The sweet scent of pine from the Christmas tree.

He loved his life. He loved his daughter. And for a split second this afternoon, he'd stood on the verge of losing it all. When the roof had collapsed and blocked his exit, he'd thought his time was up. But Mitch and Josh had gotten him out. The rescue had been nothing short of a miracle.

Seth drew a shaky breath and closed his eyes. Thank You, God.

"Seth?"

Even if he hadn't heard her voice or opened his eyes, the scent of her perfume would have told him Lauren stood before him. Though he'd just seen her this morning, the worried look in her eyes was new, as were her clothes. Dressed casually in jeans and a University of Denver sweatshirt and with her hair pulled back in a ponytail, she looked more like a college student than a responsible nanny.

He was so thankful she was here. Oh, he knew Anna would have moved in if he'd asked, but his sister was a newlywed. Her place was with her husband.

His parents would have flown up from Florida in a heartbeat, but they were still recovering from injuries sustained in a car accident in October. Traveling back to Montana for Anna's wedding had been hard enough on them.

No, Lauren was definitely a lifesaver.

"Are you okay? Can you talk?" She stepped forward, hovering close, her expression anxious.

"I'm fine, really," he said in a voice he didn't recognize, one that brought whiskey and cigarettes to mind. "How is Dani holding up?"

Lauren hesitated. "She's worried."

By the concern in her eyes, Seth saw that his daughter wasn't the only one needing reassurance.

"I was a tad bit concerned myself." His attempt to joke fell flat. "But Doc said I'll be good as new in a week or two."

Relief filled Lauren's gaze. She stepped closer and rested her hand on his arm. "I'm so happy you're okay."

"Me, too." Seth cleared his throat, embarrassed by the tremor. "I'm glad Trenton made it out."

"Thanks to you and Mitch."

When Seth had heard the boy calling for help from the second floor, he'd known there was no time to waste. Mitch had gone in right behind him. It had taken longer than Seth had thought it would to find the boy. The panic on the twelve-year-old's face when they'd found him stumbling around, disoriented by the smoke, would be forever etched in his brain.

"When the ceiling collapsed, I realized my daughter might end up an orphan," Seth said, almost to himself. "But I had no choice. I couldn't let a child die. I had to help."

"Of course you did," Lauren said reassuringly. "And now that boy will grow into a man."

Seth rubbed his hand over his eyes, trying to erase the images of the burning house. "Is Dani in the kitchen?"

Lauren nodded. "Do you need any help walking?"

"Naw." He shook his head for emphasis. It was a mistake. The room started to spin. As he reached for the wall to steady himself, Seth realized the doctor had been right. He needed to take it slow.

Lauren's arm slipped around him, providing needed stability. He accepted her support until the room righted itself.

"I'm okay," he said, shrugging off her hold.

"I'm helping you whether you like it or not." Lauren's tone brooked no argument. "You don't want to upset Dani by collapsing at her feet."

"Anyone ever tell you you're bossy?" he muttered, but he didn't pull away when she took his arm again.

Lauren laughed, encouraged by his spunk. Seth may have gotten knocked down but he was already pushing his way up from the mat. However, the way he leaned on her as they made their way slowly to the kitchen told her he had a ways to go before he'd be at full speed.

He didn't speak during the short journey. Neither did Lauren. She knew he needed to conserve his strength—and his voice—for when he faced Dani. Thankfully the child had been so busy playing she hadn't heard the truck drive up.

Lauren stopped in the doorway to the kitchen to give Seth one last breather. Dani sat at the table playing intently with the My Little Ponies that had originally belonged to her mother.

"Dani," Lauren called out. "Look who's here."

The child turned in her seat—as much as her casts would allow—and a breathtaking expression of joy

Play the
Lucky
Hearts Game
and get...
2 FREE BOOKS and
2 FREE Mystery GIFTS...
YOURS to KEEP!

yes! I have scratched off the gold card.
Please send me my **2 FREE BOOKS** and
2 FREE Mystery GIFTS (gifts are worth about $10).
I understand that I am under no obligation to purchase
any books as explained on the back of this card.

Scratch Here!
Then look below to see what your
cards get you...**2 Free Books
& 2 Free Mystery Gifts!**

We want to make sure we offer you the best service suited to your needs. Please answer the
following question:
About how many NEW paperback fiction books have you purchased in the past 3 months?

❏ 0-2   ❏ 3-6   ❏ 7 or more

335 SDL EZLW   235 SDL EZL9

FIRST NAME   LAST NAME

ADDRESS

APT.   CITY

STATE / PROV.   ZIP/POSTAL CODE

**Visit us online at
www.ReaderService.com**

Twenty-one gets you
2 FREE BOOKS and
2 FREE MYSTERY GIFTS!

Twenty gets you
2 FREE BOOKS!

Nineteen gets you
1 FREE BOOK!

TRY AGAIN!

▼ **DETACH AND MAIL CARD TODAY!** ▼

© 2009 HARLEQUIN ENTERPRISES LIMITED. Printed in the U.S.A.
® and ™ are trademarks owned and used by the trademark owner and/or its licensee.

(S-SE-09/09)

The Reader Service—Here's how it works:

danced across her face. "Daddy, I missed you so much!"

Seth dropped Lauren's arm and moved to his daughter's side.

Tears stung Lauren's eyes as the two embraced. Seth looked strong, which should reassure Dani. But Lauren knew the strength wouldn't last. She hurried to the table and pulled out a chair so he could sit next to Dani, rather than stand.

Seth offered Lauren a grateful smile before turning his attention back to his daughter. "Have you had a good day?"

"Mmm-hmm." Dani nodded her head with such emphasis, Lauren had to smile. "I helped Aunt Anna with squares this morning. And tonight, Miss Lauren has been playing ponies with me."

Seth picked up a soft plastic horse with a cotton-candy-pink tail and body. "That sounds like fun."

Dani tilted her head and studied Seth for a moment.

Lauren could see Seth prepare himself for all the questions that were sure to come.

"You're dirty." Dani wrinkled her nose. "And you smell like smoke."

"Did Miss Lauren tell you what happened?" Seth spoke softly, his voice raspy.

Dani shrugged and was silent for a second. "She told me you were a hero. That you saved Brandon's brother from a fire."

The child lowered her gaze to the pony on the table in front of her. Her lips began to tremble and tears filled her eyes. "She said you breathed in lots and lots of smoke and had to go to the hospital. I was scared."

It took every ounce of self-control Lauren possessed not to move. Her arms ached to comfort the child. But this was Seth's time with his daughter, his chance to reassure Dani that all was still well in their little world.

"I'm sorry I worried you." Seth reached up and stroked her hair. "But I'm going to be good as new very, very soon. The doctor says I just need to take it easy for a few days."

Dani's face brightened. "You can play ponies with me. It's superfun. Miss Lauren showed me how to braid hair. I can show you."

Words tumbled out of the child's mouth one after the other, and Seth listened with a fond smile on his lips.

"Can I get you something to eat or drink?" Lauren asked when Dani finally paused to take a breath. "Dani and I had grilled ham-and-cheese sandwiches for dinner. I could make you one."

A sandwich wasn't much to smile about but Lauren couldn't keep a goofy grin from her lips. She was just so happy that he was alive.

"I'm not really hungry—"

"Still, you should eat something." She clamped her mouth shut before she started to sound like his mother.

"I'm going to wash up first." Seth brought his arm to his nose and sniffed the singed fabric. "Dani's right. I do stink."

"You smell like smoke," Lauren clarified. "You do not stink."

"Yes, he does," Dani piped up, making a pony gallop across the table.

"That clinches it." His familiar smile flashed. "Shower first. Then food."

"Are you up to showering?" She didn't want to second-guess him, but his unsteadiness in the entryway worried her.

"I have to be." Seth may have lifted his chin in a determined tilt but Lauren could see the uncertainty in his eyes. He was nowhere near as confident as he appeared. "I'll feel better once I'm clean."

Lauren thought for a moment, analyzing the problem, searching for a workable solution. "You can use the shower down here."

"But that's for Dani."

"I'm sure she'll share," Lauren said, shooting a wink at the child.

"You can have anything of mine, Daddy," Dani said. "Except for my dolls. You wouldn't like them, anyway. They're more for girls than boys."

"The bathroom has a shower chair and grab bars for Dani's injury," Lauren said. "You can sit while you're washing up. If you get light-headed, at least you won't fall."

"Miss Lauren could help you," Dani said, her eyes filled with innocence. "She could wash your back and your hair like you do for me."

Seth's cheeks darkened, and if Lauren didn't know better, she'd think the cowboy was blushing. "I can manage on my own, princess. But good suggestion."

Dani's nose wrinkled. "You better go now, Daddy. The ponies told me you're making the room smell bad."

"I'm headed there now." Using the table for leverage, Seth pushed to his feet.

Lauren narrowed her gaze. She watched the way he swayed before regaining his balance, and took note of his paleness. "Dani, will you stay at the table and play while I talk to your father?"

"Sure," Dani said, whinnying like a horse and bringing two ponies together to kiss.

"I'm just fine," Seth said quietly between gritted teeth.

Lauren slipped her arm through his, ignoring the protest.

"I can manage—"

"Look," Lauren said in the firm, no-nonsense tone she reserved for the unruly students in the classes she taught. "I'm not about to hop into the shower with you. Not even if you say pretty please. Understand?"

Seth's serious expression eased into a smile. "I don't know if I should be disappointed or relieved."

"Definitely disappointed," Lauren shot back, pleased when he laughed. Sorry when he started coughing.

Yet somehow, without her quite realizing how it had happened, they were back on their old footing. It was as if the proposition had never taken place. Her heart lifted.

The walk-in shower was off the room where Dani now slept. While Seth sat on the bed and caught his breath, Lauren checked the shower. Soap was there, but no shampoo. Unless he wanted to use Dani's Strawberry Shortcake brand. She grinned at the thought.

"I'll run upstairs and get your shampoo," Lauren said. "And some clean clothes for you."

"You don't have to—"

"No worries," Lauren said lightly. "I'll be back in a flash."

She was relieved he remained seated as she left the room. Though she was sure he'd be okay in the few minutes she'd be gone, Lauren took the stairs two at a time.

Rummaging through his closets and drawers, she found a pair of jeans and a long-sleeved cotton shirt, the same color as his eyes. She was ready to head to the bathroom for the shampoo when she realized he'd need underwear, too. Unless he was the type who liked to go commando.

The thought of his bare skin beneath tight-fitting jeans sent heat coursing through her veins. But she forced the thought aside and grabbed the first pair of boxers she found.

Minutes later, with a towel and a bottle of shampoo perched precariously atop the stack of clothes, Lauren returned to Seth.

He was still sitting where she'd left him and she was pleased to see that some color had returned to his cheeks. When he'd first arrived, she'd been so happy to see him that she thought he looked wonderful. Now she realized Dani had been right.

His dark blond hair was a dusty gray. They must have washed his face at the medical center because it was clean, but his neck still held a coat of grime, as did his clothes.

She'd barely entered the room when he began coughing again. By the time the jag ended, what little color he'd gained had left his face.

"I'm putting the shampoo in the shower where it'll be easy to reach." Lauren tried not to let her apprehension show. Was he really strong enough to shower by himself? "I'll make sure the sprayer is right next to the chair and the water isn't too hot."

"Thanks, Lauren." Seth offered her a wan smile. "Forget what I said earlier. I'm not sure I could do this without you."

Instead of finding the comment reassuring, Lauren's fears escalated. He must be feeling pretty bad to admit he needed assistance.

"We need to get you undressed." Lauren placed her hands on her hips. "Can you get those jeans off yourself or do you want my help?"

Chapter Ten

Seth wasn't sure he'd heard correctly. After all, hadn't he made it clear in the kitchen that he'd be showering alone? Still, an enticing image of the two of them, naked beneath a stream of water, flashed before him. For a second he was tempted to reconsider.

"You're not coming in with me." He spoke quickly before he could weaken.

"Oh, darn. It would have been so much fun," Lauren said flippantly, snapping her fingers. "Especially with you at the top of your game."

He wasn't sure how debilitated she thought he was, but the part of him straining against the zipper of his jeans wasn't showing any sign of weakness.

"And just to clarify, I'm not planning on stripping you down naked," Lauren continued, her tone now matter-of-fact. "I'll help you with your boots, pants and shirt. Beyond that, cowboy, you're on your own."

Seth considered his options. Though he tried hard to hide it, he hadn't felt this exhausted since Dani's baby days. While he wanted nothing more than to crawl into bed, he knew he'd sleep better if he got the grime off his skin. And he wasn't sure why he was making such a big deal out of nothing. Having Lauren see him in his underwear was really no different than her seeing him at the pool.

But by the time she'd pulled off his boots and peeled off his socks, by the time she'd slipped his shirt over his head, by the time he'd unbuckled his belt and kicked off his jeans, he realized that undressing before an attractive woman in a bedroom was *very* different from being at a crowded community pool with swim trunks on.

The situation was awkward to say the least. The last time he'd worn so few clothes had been in front of his wife, and that had been a long time ago.

When it came to lovemaking, Jan had never been very adventurous. She'd preferred the lights off. And even as close as they'd been, he couldn't recall her ever staring at his body in open admiration, as Lauren was doing right now. But concern quickly replaced admiration. Her brows furrowed. "Those are a couple of mean-looking scratches."

Unexpectedly she leaned forward. When her fingers touched his skin, he jumped.

"I'm sorry." Lauren immediately straightened, her expression contrite. "I should have realized they'd be tender."

Seth didn't bother to tell her that the scrapes weren't the problem. When her fingers slid gently across his abdomen, arrows of heat had shot straight to his groin. Now his body threatened to betray him. To stop from embarrassing them both, Seth grabbed the towel and held it in front of him.

"I'll put some antiseptic on them once you get out of the shower," Lauren said.

"We'll see."

"Yes, we will see," Lauren said, her chin set in a determined tilt. "I'll be right outside. Call if you need anything."

Once the door clicked shut, he removed the last of his clothing and stepped into the shower. Even if the cuts were bleeding profusely, Lauren wasn't coming anywhere near his bare skin.

Not because he didn't trust her.

But because he didn't trust himself.

Chapter Eleven

Lauren cast one final look in her bedroom mirror. It was hard to believe the year was coming to a close. Last New Year's Eve she'd been partying with her friends at a Denver club. This year she and Seth would be attending a get-together at the Sweet River community center. Though she wasn't sure he should be going to the New Year's Eve dance, he was determined to attend. She had to admit he'd been a model patient these past five days. The results were amazing. His cough had all but disappeared and while his voice still had a distinct raspy quality, he was sounding more like the old Seth every day.

She glanced at the jean skirt and sweater she'd borrowed from Anna to wear tonight. Only in Sweet River would the attire for an end-of-the-year party be so casual. Still, her boots were more comfortable than heels and the sweater and skirt warmer than the wrap-around party dress she'd worn last year.

And Dani, well, she hadn't seemed to mind that they'd be gone. Her former babysitter had arrived fifteen minutes ago, bringing along her twelve-year-old granddaughter. Even supercautious Seth felt confident the two could meet Dani's needs for one night.

"Lauren." Seth's voice carried up the stairs. "Are you about ready?"

The fact he called to her rather than making the trek to the second floor to ask confirmed her suspicions that he wasn't quite at full speed yet.

Lauren opened the bedroom door. "I'll be right down."

It was her fault they were running late. Several months ago she'd started taking a few shifts a week on a teen crisis line. The calls were forwarded to her cell phone. Her shift was supposed to end at six today, but the last call had come in right before her time was up.

The young girl had recently broken up with an abusive boyfriend and needed reassurance that she'd made the right decision. It had been almost six-thirty before the call had ended.

Lauren smiled, remembering how much stronger the girl had sounded when she'd hung up. Though Lauren loved research and her time in the classroom, nothing matched the joy of helping someone through a crisis.

"Lauren?"

With a twinge of chagrin, she realized that during the time she'd been patting herself on the back, Seth had been patiently waiting.

"Coming." Lauren headed for the stairs, a bounce in her step.

This had been a wonderful year and in many ways she hated to see it end. But when she reached the bottom step and saw Seth's smile, she realized that the best might be yet to come.

Seth wheeled the truck onto the highway leading to town and cast a sideways glance at Lauren. When she'd glided down the stairs dressed for the evening's festivities in a skirt and sweater, he'd been shocked by his body's response.

Though she couldn't have been more covered up—with boots to her knees, a skirt that fell to her calves and a sweater that only hinted at the curves beneath—the casual, simple look was totally sexy. He liked that she'd let her hair hang loose. Not because *he* preferred it that way, but because he wanted those at the party to see what had been right in front of them all these months. Everyone was always talking about how pretty Anna and Stacie were, when Lauren was more beautiful than either of them.

"We should be there in plenty of time," Seth said in the comfortable silence that had filled the cab of the truck. "Of course, since it's a buffet, it doesn't really matter."

Normally there was only snack food at the annual New Year's Eve dance. The buffet had been a last-minute addition, a fund-raiser to help Cassie and her boys replace their personal belongings lost in the fire. Henry Millstead had donated the beef while local business owners had chipped in for the side dishes.

Stacie, Anna and other women in the community had helped with the preparation.

"If we're late, it's my fault." A tiny smile hovered at the corners of Lauren's lips, her tone holding no apology. "But I don't regret taking that last call."

Though she'd gone into the other room for the conversation, Seth had still heard bits and pieces.

"You have such a calming manner," Seth said. "I'm sure you're a really good counselor."

Unlike his sister, who could be hyper at times, or Stacie, who was as flighty as they came, Lauren's quiet confidence had the power to defuse even the most stressful situation. Like after the fire. She'd stepped up and done what needed to be done.

"I love helping people," Lauren admitted. "And it's not a one-way street. Each person teaches me something, too."

"Well, the crisis line is lucky to have you." Seth kept his eyes firmly fixed on the road, finding the emotions rising up inside him disturbing. Lust, he could understand. But these tender feelings had come out of nowhere, blindsiding him.

"One-to-one counseling is my passion...or as Stacie would say, my bliss." Thankfully oblivious to the storm raging inside him, Lauren continued telling him how much the opportunity to help those going through difficult times meant to her. Her eyes sparkled and a smile seemed to have taken up permanent residence on her lips.

Seth found it difficult to keep his eyes on the road. When they reached the street heading to the community center, he wished he could keep driving. He didn't need to talk to anyone else, laugh with anyone else. Everything he wanted was right in the cab of this truck.

Everything he wanted?

No, being with Lauren was relaxing, that was all.

As they approached the community center, Lauren leaned forward. "Look at all the cars."

Seth had been thinking the same thing, although with much less enthusiasm. "I'm not going to be able to park close. How 'bout I drop you off at the door and we reconnect inside?"

It was the gentlemanly thing to do, but Seth found himself hoping she'd refuse. It wouldn't be that far to walk. She wore boots, not spiky heels. And though there was a chill in the air, it wasn't cold. He pictured taking her arm, just in case she'd slip....

"Super idea," she said with an enthusiasm that shattered the image in his mind. "It'll give me a chance to see if Anna or Stacie needs help."

"That's what I thought." Seth kept his voice even and stopped the truck. "Hold steady. I'll get your do—"

"I've got it covered." Lauren unclasped her seat belt and pushed the door open herself. "And I'll just buy my ticket on the way in."

The dinner and dance had a suggested twenty-dollar donation. Seth had planned to pay for her admission as a token of thanks for the extra work she'd put in the past few days. Now her words had blown that all to hell. Was nothing going to go his way this evening? "Save me a seat?"

"You got it." Lauren winked and stepped from the truck. "See you inside."

The driver behind him honked. Lauren slammed the door shut and Seth shifted the truck into gear and headed up the street, his heart a little heavier than it had been only a few minutes before.

Still, it made sense Lauren would go in by herself. And pay for her own ticket. By doing so, she would be making a statement. Ensuring no one would get the wrong impression and think they were on a *date*. It was a smart move. In a town of Sweet River's size you couldn't be too careful.

What he couldn't figure out was why he was so bummed. It must simply be that he'd gotten used to having her by his side. That's why he felt strange parking the truck and walking into the party alone— something he'd done for the last three years without a second thought.

And that had to be why his heart stopped beating when he saw Lauren talking with Adam Nordstrom. Not because she was his date, or because he felt closer to her than he had to any woman other than his wife, but simply because he'd gotten accustomed to having her with him.

Lauren spotted Seth the minute he walked into the building.

After arriving, she'd been assured by her friends that they had everything under control, so she'd saved two seats at a large round table then gone in search of something to drink. That's when she'd run into Adam.

Unlike the majority of men in the room, Adam had

eschewed jeans for a pair of charcoal dress slacks and a button-down shirt, sport coat and tie. He looked very stylish and would have fit in perfectly at any of the parties she used to attend in Denver. Here, he stuck out like a sore thumb.

"I bet you can't wait to get back to civilization." Adam handed her a plastic cup filled with beer and kept one for himself.

"I guess." That's when Lauren noticed Seth, and she wondered if it'd be too bold to wave to him. Only one thought held her back. Just because he'd told her to save him a seat didn't mean he wanted to spend the entire evening with her hanging on to his coattails.

And what coattails they were. Although he was wearing jeans—along with ninety-nine percent of the men in the room—his dark brown corduroy jacket dressed up the outfit just enough.

And not only did he look great, she knew he smelled heavenly. In fact, several times on the drive into town, she'd started to compliment him on his cologne. Thankfully she'd stopped herself just in time. The last thing she wanted was for him to think she was coming on to him. Or that she considered tonight's function to be a date.

"Looks like Anderssen has arrived." Adam's expression was as unreadable as his eyes. "I assume you're sitting with him for dinner."

"He asked me to save him a seat." Lauren's stomach tightened into a knot as Seth stopped to talk to a pretty brunette. Shoving aside her irritation, she pulled her attention from the handsome rancher and refocused on the man at her side. "But there were plenty of extra seats at the table. Why don't you join us?"

* * *

The prime rib was top quality and expertly prepared but Seth's appetite had vanished the moment Adam had sat down next to Lauren.

Since Adam had come alone, Seth couldn't fault Lauren for inviting him to sit with them. It had been the hospitable thing to do. It was that same spirit that had sparked his own invitation. When he'd seen Kimberly Sizemore looking for a place to sit, he'd invited her to join them.

He'd known Kim casually for almost a year, ever since she'd first moved to Sweet River to handle the payroll and accounting for Henry Millstead's dude ranch. Their paths had crossed at several parties, and during those conversations he'd learned she was having difficulty adjusting to small-town life. Friends were in short supply. Boyfriends nonexistent.

When Lauren had first started her compatibility surveys, Seth had hoped Kim would get matched. On more than one occasion she'd hinted that one of the reasons she'd moved to Montana was to find someone special.

"Was it hard for you to leave Kansas City and move to Sweet River?" Adam asked Kim.

It was the opportunity Seth had been waiting for. All through dinner, Adam had had Lauren's undivided attention. Of course, much of that had to do with Adam. Whenever Seth would even open his mouth to say something to Lauren, Adam would hit her with another question. But over the past ten minutes it had become increasingly apparent—at least to Seth—that Lauren was tiring of the game. He'd noticed she'd begun answering Adam's questions with one-syllable responses and her gaze kept wandering.

Adam had finally gotten the message, though when the professor turned his attention to Kim, it seemed to be more in an attempt to make Lauren jealous than out of real interest in the shy accountant.

Seth wasn't about to wait around and see if it worked. This was his window of opportunity and he was seizing it. He pushed back the metal folding chair, stood and extended his hand to Lauren. "Dance with me?"

She leaned close and he caught a whiff of her perfume—the same sultry scent that had driven him crazy on the car ride over.

"Are you sure you feel up to it?" Lauren whispered against his ear.

Her words would have been disheartening except for the fact that she'd already risen to her feet and put her hand in his.

"It's a slow one." Gazing into her emerald eyes, his heart skipped a beat. Though they'd been here for over an hour, it felt as if the party was finally getting started. "You can hold me up."

Lauren chuckled and tightened her grip on his hand.

His spirits soared. When they reached the dance floor and he pulled her close, his body hummed with excitement. They swayed in silence for a minute before Lauren leaned back in his arms.

"How well do you know Kim?" she asked.

Seth lifted a shoulder in a slight shrug. "We've talked at a couple parties. I think she's pretty lonely. Moving here has been quite an adjustment for her."

"Why do you think that is?" Lauren asked, sounding truly interested.

Seth thought for a moment. "She's a nice person, but not very outgoing. That makes it hard for her to meet new people and make friends."

"I hope I get the chance to visit with her," Lauren said with a rueful smile. "I tried to at the table, but Adam was into playing twenty questions."

If she was fishing for his opinion of the professor's behavior, Seth wasn't biting.

"I think you'd like Kim," he said instead.

Lauren bit her lip and gazed up at him through lowered lashes. "Think she's interested in you?"

For a second Seth was struck dumb. He hadn't expected that question from Lauren. Josh had once teased that Kim had the hots for him, but that was just *Josh* being a guy.

"She may have been interested at one time," he said slowly. "But I didn't give her any encouragement and it never went further."

"So she didn't make a fool of herself and proposition you." Though the words were light and teasing, the hitch in Lauren's voice told him the incident between the two of them still weighed on her mind.

"That's because I didn't lead her on," Seth said. "My actions led you to draw the wrong conclusion. I was feeling that electricity, too, and I let it affect me."

"I'm feeling the sizzle now," Lauren said.

"Me, too," Seth concurred. "But look how well we're handling it."

He expected her to laugh or say something smart.

Instead her eyes narrowed and her hand curved around his arm. "I don't like the looks of that."

Seth turned and followed the direction of her gaze. Adam was helping Kim put on her coat and they were both laughing. "It's good to see her having fun for a change. What's the problem?"

"I'm just not sure what he's up to." Lauren tilted her head and her expression turned pensive. "I don't know Adam well, but I don't think he's interested in her."

"How can you know that?"

"Because he asked *me* out."

Chapter Twelve

Seth stumbled on the dance floor but quickly brought his footwork and his emotions under control. "When?"

"Pardon me?"

For a second Seth considered dropping the subject. What Lauren did on her own time was none of his business. On the other hand, she *was* living under his roof, if only temporarily. That meant he had an obligation, no, a duty to protect her from men like Nordstrom. "When did he ask you out?"

"Shortly before you walked in," Lauren said, pulling her gaze from the couple who were now walking out the door. "Jacob Weitzelman, a well-known psychologist, will be speaking in Bozeman next weekend. Adam thought I might like to see him."

"What did you tell him?"

The band shifted into another romantic ballad, but Seth didn't mind, especially when Lauren rested her cheek against his chest.

"I told him I needed to check with you first," she said.

Seth chuckled. "I bet he loved that."

"Not so much," Lauren said with a laugh.

He tightened his fingers around hers, and they swayed as one on the dance floor. "Did you tell him that to get out of going or because you really did want to check?"

She lifted her head. "If I hadn't wanted to go, I'd have said no."

Seth's heart plummeted to the tips of his cowboy boots, but when he spoke his tone was measured and businesslike. "Let me know the date and time. I'll make sure I'm home."

"Are you sure? I know you're getting better every day but—"

"I'm positive." Seth was positive, all right. Positive he didn't want her going out with Adam. Yet equally positive he had no right to stand in her way.

It was barely past ten when Lauren asked Seth if he was ready to head home. Lines of fatigue edged his eyes and his skin had taken on a dusky pallor. She was relieved when he said yes. After saying his goodbyes— and being razzed for heading home with the seniors— Seth left to get the truck.

Lauren lingered behind, wishing friends and acquaintances—and even people she didn't know—a happy New Year before heading outside. She must have stayed longer than she realized because Seth's truck was waiting at the curb when she walked out.

Her heart did a two-step. Being so close to him all evening had been unbelievably weird. Though she'd felt a definite pull, Seth had seemed totally unaffected. She'd wondered if—and had secretly hoped—he'd protest when she'd mentioned her "date" with Adam. Instead he'd given her the time *and* his blessing.

With a resigned sigh she reached for the passenger's-side door handle only to have Seth appear and open it with a flourish.

Strangely touched by the chivalrous gesture, she impulsively brushed a kiss on his cheek. "Thank you, kind sir."

"There's a time and a place for that," a voice called out from the shadows. "And a public venue isn't the time or the place."

When she'd left the center, Lauren hadn't noticed anyone on the sidewalk. If she had, she wouldn't have given Seth the friendly peck. In a town like Sweet River, even an innocent gesture could be misconstrued, especially by some of the town gossips.

Her heart dropped as Loretta Barbee stepped from the shadows into the golden glow of the streetlight. Lauren had heard an earful from both Stacie and Anna about the pastor's wife. But she hadn't been on the receiving end of the woman's meddling nature until recently.

"Evening, Mrs. Barbee." Seth rocked back on his bootheels, looking remarkably relaxed. "Happy New Year."

"Happy New Year, Seth." The woman's icy disapproval thawed under the rancher's boyish charm. "I'm glad you're feeling better. I hope to see you and Dani in church on Sunday."

Seth grinned. "Barring any more unforeseen calamities, we should be there."

"And what about you, Lauren?" The woman pinned her with a beady-eyed gaze. "Will you be there?"

Taking her cue from Seth, Lauren smiled warmly at the woman. "Wouldn't miss it."

Unfortunately the effect was ruined when the words came out in a squeak. She cleared her throat to try again. But Loretta Barbee had already spun on her heel and gone back inside.

"Happy New Year," Lauren called to the now-shut door.

"I'm afraid she can't hear you," Seth said. "On the plus side, that means she can't hear us. And for that we should be very, very glad."

His ghoulish whisper brought a smile back to her lips as she climbed into the truck. Even though she was positive—well, *almost* positive—Loretta was gone, Lauren waited until Seth was back in the driver's seat before speaking. "Had you noticed her standing in the shadows?"

"I didn't." Seth shifted and pointed the truck toward home. "But I wasn't surprised to see her. That woman has a knack for showing up where you least expect her."

He flipped the heater to high and warm air filled the cab of the truck. Lauren settled back against the seat and banished the pastor's wife to the far reaches of her mind. Perhaps it was the two beers she'd drunk. Or the fact she and Seth were finally alone. Whatever the reason, she felt wonderfully content.

She loved parties, loved seeing and talking to everyone, loved reconnecting with old friends and making new ones. But she liked this kind of one-to-one conversation, and being part of a couple, more.

Okay, so she wasn't really part of a couple. Still, when she was with Seth, the connection seemed more personal than just business. And when they were home with Dani at the kitchen table or reading books in front of a fire, it was as if she was part of a family, *his* family.

It was a household vastly different from the one she'd grown up in. When Dani talked, Seth listened. He always appeared genuinely interested in what the little girl had to say, and that interest extended to Lauren, as well. She'd never had such a home life. Her parents had always talked *at* her rather than *to* her.

"Penny for your thoughts." Seth's words broke through her reverie.

Lauren shifted in her seat to face him. "I was just thinking how much I enjoy being part of your family."

A look of surprise crossed his face.

"This has been such a great break for me," Lauren said quickly, backtracking.

"Are you still planning to take a position on the East Coast?"

"That's the plan," Lauren said. "My father has a lot of contacts and he's been putting out feelers."

"Adam Nordstrom is at Brown." Seth's eyes remained on the road. "Do you see him fitting into your future plans?"

They'd long ago left the lights of Sweet River behind. In the dimness of the truck cab, it was difficult to read Seth's expression. Lauren shrugged. "Hard to say. One thing's for sure, my father would approve."

Her lips couldn't help but curve into a smile. Another black mark against Adam.

"Your dad would hate me."

Lauren tried to envision her father and Seth in the same room. The picture refused to come into view. Probably because she knew the meeting would never happen. "It doesn't matter what he would think of you."

"Why do you say that?"

She met his gaze. "You're unavailable."

"You're right," Seth said brusquely. "It doesn't matter."

She had the feeling she'd offended him, though she wasn't sure how. But before she could ask he punched a couple of buttons on the steering wheel and turned up the radio volume. The station was a popular one, playing "all love songs, all the time."

The smooth tones of Barry Manilow filled the cab of the truck. Lauren leaned back and let the music wash over her. Back-to-back Barry tunes were interspersed with several commercials. Lionel Ritchie had just begun to sing when Lauren saw it.

Up ahead.

On the edge of the road.

A dark shape just to the right of the headlight beams. The size of a bag of laundry.

"What is that?"

When Seth glanced her way she pointed to the object. They were still too far away to identify it, but when it moved, a frisson of fear shot up her spine. That was no discarded laundry.

The smile that had been on Seth's lips vanished.

"I'm not sure." He slowed the truck and wheeled it to the side of the road. "But we're about to find out."

Chapter Thirteen

Seth was out of the truck before Lauren even unbuck-led her seat belt. She ran to catch up with him. The wind's icy fingers clawed at her face and her worry escalated with each step. Whatever was on the ground had to be nearly frozen.

"Oh, no."

It wasn't so much what Seth said, but the compas-sion in his voice that told her this was serious.

In seconds, she stood at his side. But when she glanced down, her heart rose to her throat. The animal's hair was matted with blood from a large laceration.

"Oh, no," she echoed.

Though Lauren was no animal expert, the black-and-white dog huddled on the shoulder of the road appeared to be some sort of collie.

"What do you think happened?" Lauren wasn't sure why she was whispering. They were the only people around for miles.

A muscle in Seth's jaw jumped, and in the dim light his blue eyes were gunmetal gray. "My guess is someone dumped him and he got hit by a car."

"Who would leave him way out here?" Lauren's voice rose then broke. She glanced around, taking in the pastureland that seemed to go on forever. "It doesn't make sense."

"Dumping domesticated animals in the country happens more than most think," Seth said through gritted teeth.

"But there's nothing for him to eat." The food Lauren had consumed earlier turned to stone in her stomach. "Or drink."

"I know." Seth blew out a harsh breath. "This fella didn't stand a chance."

The finality in his voice scared her.

"We can't leave him here." Lauren clenched her hands into fists.

The animal turned his head and met Lauren's gaze. When he thumped his tail against the ground, tears sprang to her eyes.

"I wouldn't think of leaving him." Seth squatted next to the dog but made no move to touch him. "I need you to go to the truck, grab a blanket from the backseat and a flashlight from the glove compartment."

Lauren hesitated. "Shouldn't we get him into the truck? Out of the weather?"

"This animal is hurt. I'm not sure how badly. I want to check him out first." Seth brushed the snow from his face with an impatient gesture. His frown deepened when the dog shivered. "But we do need to move him as soon as possible."

Lauren ran to the truck. By the time she returned Seth's hands were already moving over the dog with a confidence that brought her a measure of comfort.

He took the flashlight and shone the light into the animal's eyes and ears before checking his mouth.

Lauren raised the collar of her jacket as the snow continued to fall. "How is he?"

"Doesn't appear to have any bleeding from the nostrils or ears. Gums are pink. Pupils are reactive and equal. Other than the nasty laceration, the only thing that worries me is his back leg. It appears to be just a sprain, but I'd feel better if I had an X-ray."

Seth took the blanket from her hands and wrapped it around the animal.

"Where's the nearest vet?" Lauren asked.

"Big Timber," Seth said. "But Doc Burkey is visiting family in Phoenix."

"Then we'll take him somewhere else."

"No vet is going to be in the office on New Year's Eve." Seth handed Lauren the flashlight and lifted the dog into his arms. "We'll take him home. I'll see what I can do."

In the short time since they'd stopped, the wind had picked up and the snow had begun to fall in earnest. Lauren hurried ahead of Seth and opened the door to the backseat. With a gentle touch, he laid the dog on the leather with the blanket wrapped around him.

Bile rose in her throat. "He wouldn't have lasted much longer."

"Not in this weather," Seth agreed.

"But he'll be okay, right?" Growing up, Lauren had never had a pet. Animals, according to her parents, were messy and unnecessary. She was surprised she felt such an affinity for this one.

"If he doesn't have any internal injuries, I'd say yeah, he'll make it." The matter-of-fact tone was at odds with the worry in Seth's eyes. He slipped the phone from his pocket. "Mind if I make a quick call?"

"Not at all."

It didn't take her long to figure out that he'd rung the house to check on Dani. After a few questions, he explained about the dog. "We'll go straight to the clinic, so don't worry when you hear the truck drive up."

He flipped shut the phone and smiled. "Dani was asleep by nine."

While he drove, Seth updated her on the little girl's evening. Lauren kept one eye on the collie. Though it seemed to take forever, they finally pulled into the lane leading to the ranch.

Seth didn't spare the house a second glance. Instead he wheeled the truck in front of the metal outbuilding and shut off the engine.

In seconds he'd unlocked the door and returned to the truck for the dog. Lauren followed him to a room in the back.

"This is amazing." Lauren glanced around the spotless interior. "It's like your own vet clinic."

Seth had already placed the animal on the metal exam table and was busy pulling supplies from the cabinets.

"When Dad had the building put up, it was with the

knowledge that he and Mom would eventually be moving south and I'd be taking over the ranch," Seth explained. "He thought it would be convenient for me to have my veterinary practice right on the property. Since I didn't finish the program, I've never fully utilized this portion of the building."

An hour later Seth had cleaned the debris from the laceration and sutured it shut.

Lauren frowned as he carefully inspected the animal's hind leg. "How bad is it?"

"There's some swelling," Seth said. "But the joint seems strong and functional."

"And that tells us…"

"That it's probably not broken. And I don't think he damaged any ligaments." Relief flowed through his voice. "We should be okay with some anti-inflammatory medications and a short-term splint."

Seth gave the sedated dog a pat and grabbed a bandage from the cabinet. He bent over the exam table where the dog lay snoring and began wrapping the bandage around the injured leg. "Not fancy but it'll do."

Since he'd used the ether sparingly, by the time Seth secured the bandage, the animal was already stirring.

Lauren glanced about the room. "Where will he sleep tonight?"

Seth leaned over and pulled a large wire cage from under the counter. "This should work."

Lauren's heart sank. She'd pictured the collie on one of those fluffy dog beds she'd seen on television, not in a wire prison. "I hate to see him in a *cage*."

"If he has too much freedom he could reinjure himself." With expert hands, Seth settled the animal inside the cage, latched the door and straightened. "Give him a little time and he'll be good as new."

His gaze locked with hers and she saw gratitude—and some other emotion she couldn't identify—in the liquid blue depths.

"Thanks for sticking around," he said. "Having that extra pair of hands really helped."

Unexpected warmth flowed through her. While she'd always received kudos for her academic achievements, this one was personal. "My pleasure."

"What a way to spend New Year's Eve." Though Seth shook his head, a tiny smile played at the corners of his lips.

"I can't imagine a better way to end a year." Lauren gazed at the sleeping dog and her heart swelled with emotion. "It's not often I get to help save a life."

"It feels good."

"Good? That word hardly seems adequate."

"You're right." Seth grinned. "There's nothing like it."

"You've got a gift, Seth." She touched his arm. "You should be so proud of yourself, of what you did here tonight."

The tips of his ears turned red, but she barely noticed. It was his eyes that held her mesmerized. The emotion she'd noticed before had returned, only stronger and more easily recognizable. Her body responded, sending heat thrumming through her veins. Despite the late hour, she was suddenly wide-awake.

"I suppose we should head inside," she said, shifting from one foot to the other, waiting for him to make his move. And waiting. And waiting some more.

His eyes darkened. For a second she thought he was going to kiss her again. Instead he moved to the stainless-steel sink, turning his back to her. She watched silently as he took an inordinate amount of time washing his hands. When he turned back surprise flashed in his eyes. It was as if he hadn't expected to see her still standing there.

"I need to get some ice on his leg," he said brusquely. "And I'll have to continue with the neuro checks. Make sure there's no brain injury. The signs don't always show up right away."

"Then I'll stay and keep you company," Lauren began to offer, but he started shaking his head before she'd even finished speaking.

"You'll have Dani to care for in the morning." He wiped his hands on a paper towel and tossed it into the waste can. "You need your sleep."

"But what about you?" For a second concern replaced desire. "You're still recovering from the—"

Without warning he stepped close and pressed a finger against her lips. "I'll be fine."

Her heart fluttered in her chest like a trapped butterfly. Though his hand dropped back to his side, his gaze remained focused on her.

Seth had long ago discarded his jacket and rolled up the sleeves of his shirt. Stubble covered his cheeks and signs of fatigue edged his eyes.

In her mind he'd never looked sexier. The fact that he would stop and care for an injured animal with such compassion only added to his appeal.

Ignoring the red flags popping up in her head, Lauren took a step forward and placed the flat of her hand against his chest. She could feel the solid thud of his heartbeat beneath her palm, the heat of his skin through the fabric of his shirt. So she was playing with fire. Send her to hell. The desire that flared in Seth's eyes told her louder than any words that she wouldn't be heading there alone.

It was that realization that gave Lauren the confidence she needed to slide her hands up his back and twine them together behind his neck. He was now so close she could see the flecks of gold in his smoldering eyes. He smelled of soap and an infinitely warm male scent that made something tighten low in her abdomen.

But before she could make another move, a tinny version of "Auld Lang Syne" filled the air.

"What is that?" Seth's gaze never strayed from hers.

"I set the alarm on my phone for midnight." Her pulse seemed to stall, then thump like a bass drum. "Happy New Year, Seth."

"Happy New Year, Lauren." He didn't smile, but simply stood there looking at her, his eyes shadowed and unreadable.

She wasn't sure who broke the stalemate. She wasn't sure it mattered. All she knew was that his lips were finally, blessedly, locked with hers.

Lauren couldn't remember ever having been kissed quite like this before. It started out slowly but changed the moment Seth's tongue swept across her lips.

Her hands dropped from his neck and she curled her fingers in the fabric of his shirt. Everything faded except the need to feel more of him, taste more of him, touch more of him.

When he pulled her close and his erection pressed against her belly, a dizzying myriad of sensual images of the two of them together flashed before her.

As he continued to scatter kisses along her jawline, a shivering, sliding sensation ran down her spine. Her breasts strained against the sweater and she heard herself groan, a low sound of want and need that astonished her with its intensity.

Without warning, Seth released his hold and stepped back. For a second Lauren thought he might kiss her again. Until she lifted her eyes to his face…and saw the regret.

Seth took a couple of deep breaths and fought to gain control of his rioting emotions. Lauren's groan had been a wake-up call. Somehow he'd let things get out of control.

Unexpectedly her arms looped around his neck and she inclined her head, resting her forehead against his.

"No regrets, bub," she said in a soft, low voice that told him she'd managed to read his mind. "I don't have any and you shouldn't, either."

"This shouldn't have happened." Seth lifted his head and stared into her emerald eyes. He never lost control. Never.

"It was a *kiss*." Lauren smiled softly. "The tension that had been building between us needed an outlet. End of story. Nothing to beat yourself up over."

She leaned forward and kissed him gently on the cheek. "I should go inside. Relieve the babysitter."

Lauren lifted her coat from the hook by the door. He

moved to her side and helped her into it, but he pulled his hands away when they wanted to linger.

"Where do we go from here?" he heard himself asking.

"Back to me being the nanny and you being Dani's dad," Lauren said coolly. "It was simply a kiss. No big deal."

Seth woke the next morning feeling as if he had a two-thousand-pound bull sitting on his chest. He rolled over and grabbed the inhaler from the bedside stand. Pushing himself to a sitting position, he inhaled two puffs of the medicine.

He ignored the panicky feeling and waited for the medicine to work its magic. After a minute, his lungs opened up and his breath came easily, allowing him to relax and enjoy the sunlight streaming through the window.

It was amazing how much light there was for so early in the day. Seth glanced at the clock. He blinked once. Then blinked again. He couldn't remember the last time he'd slept until eleven. It had to have been back in college. Before he had responsibility for the ranch and a child, and now an injured dog.

A dog that was probably wide-awake and ready to be let out of his crate.

Seth pulled on his clothes in record time, but when he reached the stairs, he slowed his pace. He'd learned it didn't take much exertion to bring on the coughing. By the time he cleared the bottom step, his breath was coming in shallow puffs. He rested with one hand on the banister until he heard voices coming from the back of the house, and he followed the sounds to the kitchen.

He found his daughter seated at the table, a pre-made pizza crust in front of her, along with bowls heaped with cheese, pepperoni, green peppers and chopped-up mushrooms.

Lauren stood at the counter, studying a jar of pizza sauce. With the sunlight streaming through the window caressing her silvery-blond hair, she looked as close to an angel as he'd ever seen.

"You're awake," Dani called out. "Hooray!"

Seth shifted his focus to his daughter. Was there anything sweeter than a child's welcoming smile?

"Happy New Year, Seth." Lauren set aside the sauce and moved to the coffeepot. "One cup of your favorite Colombian blend coming right up."

"You don't have to wait on me," Seth protested.

"You're still recovering," Lauren said. "And you were up late. You deserve a little pampering."

"The coffee smells wonderful." Seth inhaled the rich aroma. "But before I do anything, I need to check on the collie."

"He's right there, Daddy." Dani pointed to the large kennel in a far corner of the kitchen. "Miss Lauren and Mr. Swenson brought him inside."

"I hope you don't mind." Lauren poured the steaming brew into a cup and brought it to him. "It was snowing hard this morning. I thought having him in the house would make it easier for you to monitor him."

"Thank you, Lauren." Seth wrapped his hands around the mug and took a sip. He glanced down at the cup. "I bet I'm not the only one who's thirsty. Before I sit down I'd better get the dog water."

"We gave him some already," Dani said. "He drank and drank and drank. He was a thirsty boy. Then we, well, Miss Lauren took him outside so he could do his business."

Seth smiled at her enthusiasm. The love of animals was something he and Dani shared. "Sounds like you took good care of him." He shifted his gaze to include Lauren. "Thank you."

Her cheeks pinked in a charming blush, just as they had when he'd kissed her.

"I read to him," Dani said. "He likes Junie B. Jones as much as I do."

"Dani is a good little reader," Lauren told Seth, shooting Dani a wink. "And she's a great help. She read to our injured pup while I got the ingredients together for the pizza."

"We make a good team." From the way Dani made the pronouncement, Seth had the feeling she was repeating what Lauren had said to her.

Dani looked so proud and content that his heart swelled with emotion. It was amazing how much happier his daughter had been since Lauren had come to live with them.

"I told Bailey you'd make sure he healed up real good," Dani added.

Seth took a seat at the table and lifted a brow. "Bailey?"

"That's what I named him," Dani said. "Miss Lauren said it suits him, whatever that means."

He smiled. "It means she thinks he looks like a Bailey."

"You will make sure he gets better, won't you, Daddy?" Dani's earnest blue eyes focused on him. "You made all the other animals better." Dani lifted a hand and counted them off. "The raccoon, the robin, the baby calf, your horse—"

"I'm impressed," Lauren said.

Seth shrugged off the compliment.

"My daddy is the bestest vet ever."

"I'm not a vet, Dani," Seth said. "Just someone who likes animals."

"You could be, you know," Lauren said in a low voice when Dani shifted her attention to Bailey.

"How could I take time away from her and the ranch to go back to school?" Seth shook his head. "At this point in my life it's not feasible."

Lauren just looked at him.

"It's important not to bite off more than you can chew." Seth wondered why it felt so much like a cop-out when he was merely stating facts. The clock in the living room began to chime and he groaned.

"What's the matter?" Lauren asked.

"Mitch and Anna's football party."

"I'd forgotten all about it." Lauren's brow rose. "When does it start?"

"An hour ago."

Chapter Fourteen

Every day for the past five days Seth had tried to convince himself the kiss was no big deal. Just a way to welcome in the new year. But no matter how many times he told himself the kiss didn't mean anything, his gut told him it did.

The more he was around Lauren, the more he liked her. He enjoyed talking to her, not only about everyday events at home but also about what was going on in the world. Her keen intellect challenged him and had actually caused him to reconsider some of his beliefs. She was fun, too. Looking back, he realized he'd laughed more during these past few weeks than he had in years. And watching Dani blossom under her attention made his heart melt.

But the more he thought about it, the more he

wondered if bringing Lauren into his household had been a mistake. If he wasn't careful, he could easily fall in love with her. "That would be a disaster."

"What would be a disaster?"

Mitch's question jerked Seth from his reverie. He'd almost forgotten his friend had insisted on accompanying him out to the stable.

Seth thought quickly. "If Star got an infection in her wound."

He picked up the bucket of supplies and headed to the stall of his favorite cutting horse.

Mitch hooked a boot on the gate. "How'd she get injured?"

The nine-hundred-pound bay tossed her head at the unfamiliar voice.

"Bumped up against a fence." Seth kept his voice calm and low. Star had been a model patient so far, but she obviously wasn't pleased he'd brought a visitor with him.

"What does she think of the new dog?"

Seth glanced down, not surprised to see the black-and-white border collie at his feet. Though it had been less than a week since he and Lauren had rescued him from the side of the highway, the animal had made a remarkable recovery. The laceration was healing without any signs of infection, and you'd never know the leg had been injured. "Bailey is good around the horses. And great around Dani."

"So you're keeping him?"

"Dani would throw a fit if I sent him away." Seth smiled remembering how her little face had lit up when he'd told her they could keep the collie. It had been like Christmas morning all over again.

With supplies in hand, Seth slipped inside the stall. "She insisted we bring him inside New Year's Day."

"Is that why you didn't come over?" Mitch asked. "Because Dani wanted to play nursemaid to a dog?"

The football party and brunch at Mitch and Anna's house had been on Seth's calendar for over a month. But when New Year's Eve had turned into an all-nighter, Seth had decided he needed a restful day at home more than he needed to socialize.

"Like I told you, I'd been up all night with Bailey." Seth set the supplies down so he could stroke Star's nose. "I wouldn't have been very good company."

"Anna was disappointed you kept Lauren home with you."

"I told her she didn't have to stick around," Seth assured his friend. "But she insisted on staying."

"Tell me you at least watched the game," Mitch said.

"I woke up just as it was starting." It hadn't taken him long to discover Lauren loved football almost as much as he did. By the third quarter any awkwardness between them had disappeared. "Lauren and Dani made pizza that morning and we ate in front of the television. After the game we had homemade ice cream to celebrate the V."

Seth carefully removed the bandage from Star's thigh and inspected the wound, but his mind kept going back to that afternoon. Lauren had never tasted homemade ice cream and it had been love at first bite. The ecstasy on her face and the sound she'd made when the creamy sweetness hit her tongue had brought all sorts of thoughts to mind, none of them G-rated.

He ignored the sensations the memory aroused and

forced his attention back to the mare. Seth felt his friend studying him as he cleansed the wound with saline and applied a fresh bandage.

"Sounds like you and Lauren are getting along pretty well," Mitch said.

"She's easy to be around," Seth admitted.

"You like her?"

"As a friend."

"Loretta Barbee saw her and Nordstrom having dinner at a restaurant in Bozeman Saturday."

Seth had tried to put that night out of his mind. He hadn't wanted Lauren to go but he'd put on a good front. He had no right to tell her who she could and couldn't associate with, even if the guy was a selfish jerk who'd only seen his father once every five years. And while that wasn't the only reason that twisted the knife in Seth's gut when she'd walked out the door, it was good enough.

"I didn't realize they were dating," Mitch added when Seth didn't immediately respond.

"It wasn't a *date*," Seth clarified. "They went to a lecture and decided to catch some dinner first."

Lauren had looked exceptionally pretty that evening. And she'd smelled even better. Seth clenched his teeth together and gathered the supplies. After giving Star one last pat, he joined Mitch outside the stall.

"You didn't want her to go."

"Didn't matter to me."

"Liar." Mitch cocked his head to the side. "I've seen the way you two look at each other. Are you sleeping with her?"

"Absolutely not." Seth yanked his coat from the

hook. That night in the clinic had been a close call. Too close.

"But you *have* kissed her."

Seth scowled. "How is that any of your business?"

"Okay, we've established that you've kissed her." A look of satisfaction crossed Mitch's face. "How was it?"

"Awkward." Seth shoved one arm and then the other into his coat sleeves.

"The ice queen cometh?"

"Not at all." Just remembering the sweet taste of Lauren's lips had the power to turn his blood into a river of molten lava. "Hot would be more the word."

Mitch's expression was clearly skeptical. "If the kiss was hot, you'd have slept with her."

"Lauren is Dani's nanny."

"Give me a better excuse."

Seth couldn't believe Mitch was being so persistent. He held on to his temper with both hands and reminded himself Mitch had no idea this was a sore subject. And if Seth didn't get all uptight, he never would. "I made a promise to Jan."

"Anna said you promised not to *marry* until Dani was grown. She didn't say anything about not sleeping with anyone." Mitch paused. "And why did you make that marriage promise again?"

Mitch had been living out of state during Jan's illness and death. Seth realized they'd never talked about that time.

"Jan's parents divorced when she five," he explained. "Her mother remarried when she was about Dani's age. To say Jan and her stepdad weren't close would be a huge understatement."

"So she made you promise because she was worried about Dani having a wicked stepmother," Mitch said matter-of-factly.

Worry over her daughter's future had consumed his wife's last days. "Jan loved Dani so much. She just wanted her to have the very best life possible."

"More parents should be that concerned." Mitch's jaw set in a hard tilt and his face became an expressionless mask. Seth had no doubt his friend was remembering his own broken and dysfunctional childhood.

Mitch pulled on his gloves and stepped outside without even zipping his coat. They were almost to the house when he stopped and faced Seth. "What I can't understand is why Jan didn't trust you."

"She trusted me."

"No, she didn't," Mitch insisted. "If she had, she wouldn't have been concerned about Dani's future. She'd have known you'd never marry anyone who didn't love your daughter."

Seth changed the subject, but for the rest of the day he couldn't stop thinking about Mitch's comment. Had Jan really not trusted him to do what was best for Dani? He'd always tried to be a good husband, a good father. Granted, he hadn't spent as much time with Dani before Jan died as he had after she'd passed. But part of that had been because of his wife. She'd been a traditionalist, believing a mother should be the primary caregiver.

Had she feared he'd marry the first woman who crossed his path just so he'd have someone to take care of Dani?

He remembered those dark days after the funeral.

The house had seemed so empty. It had been difficult to take care of the ranch, mourn the loss of his wife and try to meet the physical and emotional needs of a grieving child. Perhaps he *would* have taken the easy way out and married quickly....

Seth immediately rejected the notion. As stressful as his life had been at the time, to him marriage was sacred. Besides, it hadn't taken him long to discover that he loved being an active participant in Dani's care. In fact, even if he did marry again, he'd never go back to being on the sidelines of her life.

But because of the promise he'd made, it didn't matter if he fell in love. It didn't matter if the woman loved Dani as much as he did. It didn't matter if they could build a warm and rich life for themselves and Dani.

All that mattered was that he'd looked into Jan's eyes and made a vow. And he couldn't see how he could live with himself if he broke that promise.

Chapter Fifteen

It had been quite a week.

Lauren beat the egg mixture with a whisk and poured the liquid into a skillet. She'd made great strides in analyzing her dissertation research, Dani had started walking short distances on her rocker cast, and they'd added the adorable border collie to their household.

Every time Lauren thought about it as "their" household, she reined herself in and gave herself a stern lecture. This was Seth's household. She was merely a friend lending a hand.

The only trouble was it had started to feel like *her* home. She'd spent almost every waking moment of the past couple weeks with Seth and Dani. While Seth relaxed and continued to recover from smoke inhalation, they'd eaten breakfast, lunch and dinner together.

Every evening before Dani went to bed, Lauren and Seth took turns reading to her in front of a crackling fire with Bailey at their feet.

After Dani and Bailey went to bed, they stayed up and talked about everything from changes in the global economy to the upcoming basketball tournament at Sweet River High School.

Lauren remembered her father once remarking that if he had to spend more than five consecutive days in her mother's company he'd go crazy. She'd accepted the statement and not given it much thought. Now it made her sad. She couldn't imagine ever feeling that way about Seth.

"Stop it," she told herself.

"Stop what?"

She whirled around.

Seth leaned against the doorjamb, looking incredibly sexy in a blue plaid shirt and jeans. Today would be his first full day working the ranch. He coughed only rarely now and she hadn't heard him wheeze in days.

In honor of his recovery, Lauren had decided to fix him a big breakfast.

"Stop thinking that my scrambled eggs are ever going to be as fluffy as yours," Lauren said, improvising.

She picked up a spatula and turned her attention back to the skillet, not wanting him to see the longing in her eyes. Lauren had stayed true to her silent vow to let him make the next move, but every time he touched her hand or came close to her for any reason it took everything she had not to wrap her arms around him.

"It's all in the wrist action," he said.

She froze in place as he stood behind her and reached around so they both held the spatula. His face was next to hers, and if she turned ever so slightly, her lips would meet his. If she turned around completely, she'd be in his arms.

"Just like this." He flipped over the eggs, then stepped back.

Was it only her imagination or was his breathing suddenly as ragged as hers? She'd like to think so, but since the night they'd almost lost control, he'd been a perfect gentleman.

"Have a seat at the table." Lauren shoved aside her frustration and forced a pleasant smile. "Food is ready."

"I'll get the orange juice and coffee." Seth headed for the refrigerator, and Lauren could breathe again.

She shifted her attention to Dani, who sat at the table engrossed in the latest Junie B. Jones book. Dani had gotten up extra early and had practically inhaled her cereal so she could return to reading.

"More juice, Dani?" Lauren asked.

"No, thank you," Dani said, not looking up from the page.

Over bacon and eggs, they talked easily, as they did most mornings. But she knew Seth well enough now to tell that something was bothering him. She sipped her second cup of coffee and waited for him to tell her what was on his mind.

"I heard you're back analyzing compatibility surveys." He brought the cup to his lips and took a sip. His tone was casual, making his death grip on the cup even more puzzling. "I thought you had all the data you needed."

Lauren sat back in her chair. "Kim Sizemore hadn't been matched the first time around. She called the other day and asked if she could try again."

"What about Adam? I heard he was throwing his hat into the dating pool."

"News travels fast." The Internet had nothing on the town's gossip mill. "Who told you?"

"I ran into Loretta Barbee yesterday when Swen and I were in town getting supplies," Seth said, surprisingly serious. "Apparently Adam is convinced you and he will be a perfect match."

Lauren resisted the urge to roll her eyes. "If I was a betting woman, I'd say he'll match with Kim."

"But why would he think it could be you and him?" Seth's brows pulled together. "You never completed a survey."

"Actually I did," Lauren admitted. "Adam suggested experiencing the survey process firsthand would round out my dissertation experience. Although obviously that wasn't the reason he urged me to participate."

"But why now?" Seth's voice reflected the confusion on his face.

"Doing it earlier wouldn't have been proper protocol." Lauren took a sip of orange juice. "But since my research is complete, this is just for fun."

"I like fun." Dani looked up from her book. She'd been so quiet Lauren had forgotten she was there. "What are you doing that's for fun?"

"Just a survey," Lauren said.

Dani frowned. "What's that?"

Lauren looked at Seth, but he'd picked up the paper and was pretending to read.

"It's a bunch of questions," Lauren explained. "The answers tell me who in this area could be my good friend."

It was a simplistic explanation, hopefully easy for a seven-year-old to understand.

"It'll say me," Dani said.

"Me?" Now Lauren was the one confused.

"No, silly." Dani giggled, pointing with her cast to her chest. "It will say I'm your good friend, 'cause you and me are bestest friends."

The sincerity in the little girl's tone threaded a ribbon of love around Lauren's heart. Over the past few weeks she and Dani had grown close. And to discover the child considered Lauren to be her "bestest" friend brought a lump to her throat.

She cast a sideways glance at Seth to see if he'd heard the touching words, but his eyes were still on the paper.

"If you *could* take the survey," Lauren said to Dani, "I'm sure it would show we are meant to be best friends. But this particular survey matches men and women. It matched your aunt Anna with your uncle Mitch. And Stacie and Josh."

Dani's lips pursed together for a moment then she smiled. "And you and Daddy."

Seth choked on his sip of coffee, telling Lauren he wasn't as engrossed in the paper as he'd appeared.

"You and Daddy are bestest friends, too." Dani's smile was triumphant, as if she'd put the answer in a box, tied it with a bow and presented it to Lauren.

"You're right, princess." Seth lowered the paper to

the table. "But there are other men in town who could be Miss Lauren's good friend, too. Like Mr. Nordstrom. He and Miss Lauren have a lot in common. They both—"

"Seth." Lauren softened her interruption with a smile. She could see by the distress on Dani's face that the talk of other men was upsetting her. And for no good reason.

She might not match anyone. Look at Seth. He'd never been matched. And for all his talk about her supposed compatibility with Adam, as far as she was concerned the professor's boorish behavior on the trip they'd taken to Bozeman for the psychology lecture had disproved that assumption. He hadn't been interested in the speaker at all. In fact, he'd read e-mail on his BlackBerry during the presentation. Talking about her father all the way there and back hadn't been much fun, either. But the way he'd slammed Sweet River every chance he got had been the last straw.

"Did Mrs. Barbee also tell you Adam is doing a lecture next week at your alma mater?" Lauren asked, more than ready for a subject change.

"What about?"

Lauren shrugged. "I heard the words *cluster species* and *algorithms* and tuned him out."

Seth raised both eyebrows. "Sounds…interesting."

"Yeah, right." Lauren laughed. "Only if you're a math geek."

"Are you going?"

Lauren didn't even have to think about her answer. "You couldn't pay me enough to go."

* * *

Seth gazed into the crackling fire. His chores were all done. Dani had been in bed for hours. He assumed Lauren was asleep by now, too. She'd gone to her bedroom after dinner to work on her dissertation…and because she probably sensed he needed some time alone.

He'd been distracted all evening, but instead of badgering him to tell her what was wrong, she'd let him be.

Even if she'd asked and he'd wanted to tell her, he wasn't sure what he'd have said. All Seth knew was that ever since his conversation with Mitch several days earlier, he'd felt unsettled.

He looked up at the sound of footsteps on the stairs and his heart flip-flopped in his chest. He hadn't expected to see Lauren again this evening.

But his smile of welcome faded when he saw her tears. Seth jumped to his feet and hurried to her side. "What's the matter?"

She swiped at her cheeks with the tips of her fingers, her smile wobbly. "Sorry. I thought you'd already gone to bed."

Seth shot her a wink. "I was waiting up for you."

He was rewarded with a slight smile.

"I came down because I couldn't sleep."

Seth forced a teasing tone. "And to see me, of course."

This time the smile reached her eyes. "How'd you guess?"

He tapped his temple with an index finger. "Psychic."

She laughed and the tense set of her shoulders eased.

"Come sit with me by the fire." Sensing her embarrassment, he pretended not to notice her red-rimmed eyes.

When she hesitated, he grabbed her hand and pulled her to the sofa. "C'mon, I don't bite."

When she sat, he dropped down next to her. "Talk to me."

"About what?"

"What's keeping you from sleeping might be a good place to start."

"You mean, other than you?"

He grinned. "Other than me."

Her gaze shifted and the smile faded from her lips. Tears welled in her eyes, but she blinked them back. "My father called."

Seth shifted in his seat and took her hands, trying not to show his alarm. "What did he have to say?"

Lauren shook her head. "You should get to bed." She tried to pull her hands away, but he held on. "You're still recovering. You don't need to listen to me whine about my life. I'll just make some warm milk and—"

"Lauren," he said gently but firmly, cutting off her nervous chatter. "I can't make it better if I don't know what's wrong. Did something happen to your mother? Or your dad?"

"No. No. Nothing like that."

Seth released the breath he didn't realize he'd been holding. "Then what?"

"Okay, but please understand." A hint of pink tinged her cheeks. "I'm not some child desperate for a father's love and approval. I've known for a long time exactly where I fit into his life."

"Understood."

"I grew up with every material advantage. But now, after observing firsthand what a home filled with love looks and feels like, I realize that I was shortchanged. And it makes me angry. And hurt. And…"

As he listened to her talk, Seth realized she wasn't the only one who'd had her eyes recently opened. Lauren's presence had brought completeness to his world. While he loved the ranch and his life with Dani, there'd been an emptiness inside him.

An emptiness only Lauren had been able to fill. His gaze settled on her face. He couldn't deny it any longer. He was falling in love with her. No, he was in love with her. But instead of joy, despair flowed through his veins.

"This situation doesn't lend itself to a quick-fix solution," she added.

Truer words had never been spoken.

Seth squeezed her hands. "My grandmother used to say a burden is always lighter when it's shared with someone who…cares."

"I hadn't spoken with my father since Thanksgiving, and that was when I called him."

Seth bit his tongue and smiled encouragingly.

"Edmund didn't call me to ask about my Christmas or to see how I was doing." Though she spoke calmly, he heard the underlying hurt. "Apparently Adam had e-mailed him about his lecture in Bozeman on Monday. Since my father was already flying to the East Coast for a symposium in New York, he changed his airline reservations so he could stop over and listen."

"And so he could see you," Seth reminded her.

"Actually he made it clear he was stopping in Montana only because Adam was speaking," Lauren said lightly, her smile not reaching her eyes.

"He must think a lot of the guy." Seth couldn't think of anything else to say. Or at least anything that didn't involve a few choice cuss words.

Lauren gave a humorless laugh.

"Still, he's going to see you while he's here. I mean, he'll be just down the road."

"I asked. He hadn't built in the extra time to come all the way to Sweet River." Lauren's eyes were now dry, but the sadness lingering in the emerald depths tore his heart in two.

"Why even bother to call?" Seth asked.

"He asked if I was interested in driving to Bozeman to listen to the lecture. Said I could go to dinner with him and Adam afterward. He hinted he may have news about one of the colleges where I'd interviewed."

Seth's heart stuttered. "That's right. You'll soon be starting a whole new exciting life."

Lauren stared into the flickering flames. "I'm really going to miss it here. My clients. My work on the crisis line…everything."

What about me? he wanted to ask. Will you miss me?

"Hopefully you can still do counseling wherever you go," he said instead.

"Colleges are cutting budgets." Lauren shrugged.

"I'll have a heavy class load as well and be expected to do research and publish. I wouldn't be able to do justice to the clients."

"You'll be a great professor," Seth said. "You're someone who'll be successful at whatever you choose to do."

He gazed at her for a long moment, tempted to ask her to stay. But the words wouldn't come. She deserved so much more than a friendship or an affair. Besides, there could be no prestigious career in Sweet River. He cleared his throat. "Are you going to go to dinner?"

"Therein lies the problem," Lauren said. "A few things my father said make me think Adam is giving him the impression he and I are…involved."

"But you're not involved." Seth cleared his throat. "Right?"

Lauren jerked her hands from where they'd been sitting very nicely in his. "You know he's not my type."

Her gaze met his. Though they came from different worlds, she understood him. And he understood her. *He* was her type, not Adam Nordstrom.

No man would ever love her as much as he did. There was a certainty to the knowledge that was absolute. Even though he didn't plan to act on his feelings for Lauren, he'd go with her to the dinner, help smooth things over with her father. He'd make nice with Adam, too…even if it killed him. "What if I went with you? Would that make it easier for you?"

"You'd do that? Why?"

"Anything for a trip to Bozeman." *Anything for you.*

Lauren laughed, but quickly sobered. "What about Dani?"

"Anna and Mitch wanted to have her over sometime this week," he said. "I'll call in the morning and set it up for Monday."

"Why are you doing this?" Lauren tilted her head, her expression clearly puzzled.

"Because." He tucked a wayward curl behind her ear. "I want you to be happy."

Chapter Sixteen

Lauren's father was not at all what Seth had pictured. He'd envisioned a small man in his fifties with a mop of wiry gray hair. Instead Edmund Van Meveren was just over six feet with dark hair that was cut short. And he looked to be in his late sixties, which, now that Seth thought about it, would be about right if Lauren had been a late-in-life baby.

The lecture had been boring and attended by mostly graduate students. The restaurant Edmund had chosen was one of Bozeman's finest, aptly named the Steak House. Instead of peanut shells on the floor and plank tables, there were linen table-cloths and an extensive wine list.

For Seth, seeing the shock on Adam's face when he'd walked in at Lauren's side had made the entire trip worthwhile. Lauren's father had been polite but cool. But then he'd been distant with Lauren, too. Instead of hugging her, as Seth had expected, he'd simply shaken her hand.

Seth took a sip of iced tea and listened with one ear to the conversation. The way he saw it, he was here to lend Lauren moral support, not hijack the meeting between her and her father. That appeared to be *Adam's* role.

For the past twenty minutes Adam and Lauren's father had been talking mathematics while Seth and Lauren ate.

"I don't know if I mentioned it," Adam said, "but I had a chance to read over the compatibility survey Lauren devised for her research project. Very well done."

Edmund looked at his daughter for the first time in almost half an hour.

Though Lauren just smiled, the flare of hope in her eyes told Seth how much her father's approval meant to her.

"In fact," Adam continued, "I was so impressed I decided to fill out one of them myself."

Edmund raised a brow. "Why in the world would you do that?"

"Curiosity," Adam said. "After all, this is a dissertation project."

For a second Seth thought Edmund snorted, but then he coughed, so he wasn't sure if he'd imagined the response. Until he glanced at Lauren and saw the flash of anger in her eyes.

"Actually, sir—" Seth forced a conciliatory tone "—Lauren has had some marriages result from the survey candidates she sent on dates."

Edmund didn't acknowledge that Seth had spoken. Instead his gaze shifted to his daughter and he shook his head. "And you wonder why I don't take this discipline seriously. Your research sounds like nothing more than a matchmaking service."

Seth had been taught from an early age to respect his elders, but the patronizing tone in the older man's voice roused his protective instinct. "It's not—"

"You've missed the point." Lauren's voice was as strong and firm as the look she gave Edmund. "The weddings illustrate that the survey was a good tool for assessing compatibility. Not only were these couples compatible on paper, they fell in love."

Her father appeared to weigh her words and Seth felt a surge of hope. All the man needed to do was give Lauren a little recognition for a job well done. Surely that wasn't too much to ask.

Edmund took a sip of wine. "So who did you match with Adam? I can't believe there are many women around here who'd be *his* equal."

Seth tightened his fingers around his iced-tea glass. Apparently a little recognition *was* too much to ask.

"You forget, Professor. Your daughter lives here," Adam said, smiling at Lauren. "Surely you would find me an acceptable match for her."

Edmund placed his glass of wine on the table. His piercing gaze narrowed on Lauren. "You completed a survey? Surely you're aware this will compromise your results."

Lauren lifted her chin. "I did it *after* I'd compiled and analyzed all my data."

The fact that Lauren didn't mention Adam's encouragement to complete the survey didn't surprise Seth. He'd come to realize that Lauren was a woman who took responsibility for her actions.

"So did I match with someone?" Adam asked, his tone a shade too eager.

"You mean, did you match with *Lauren?*" Seth tried to keep the irritation from his voice, but failed. Regardless of what her father might think, this guy was not anywhere near good enough for Lauren.

Adam ignored Seth's comment.

"You did get a hit." Lauren smiled. "Kim Sizemore."

"Kim?"

Seth swore Adam's voice jumped two octaves. He took another sip of tea, the tightness gripping his chest suddenly gone.

"Why are you so surprised?" Lauren asked him. "Word around town is you've been sleeping with her. Maybe you should try taking her out on a date, even talk to her sometime. I think you'll find you have more in common than you think."

"Lauren." Edmund's voice was sharp with disapproval. "That's quite enough."

"Kim is content with our relationship the way it is," Adam said stiffly, refusing to look Lauren in the eye.

Coward, Seth thought. *Can't even be honest with himself.*

"That may be what she says," Lauren said. "But, Adam, I guarantee she wants more from you—"

"Forget about Adam's social life. Concentrate on your own future." Edmund's lips rose in a smug smile. "I have it on good authority that King's College, a small but well-respected private college in Virginia, will be offering you a position once you have your doctorate."

"Why, that's…wonderful," Lauren said.

"A friend is the chancellor there," Edmund said. "I'm certain I don't need to tell you this is an excellent opportunity."

"I realize that," Lauren said. "And I appreciate your efforts to get me that offer."

"Of course you'll accept."

"I'll certainly consider it."

"Consider?" Her father's brows pulled together like two dark thunderclouds. "What is there to consider?"

Seth couldn't believe her father didn't know. He wasn't even related to Lauren and he knew how much her crisis work and private counseling meant to her.

"It's a wonderful offer. I'd have to be crazy to turn it down," Lauren said, then immediately changed the subject to a recent accolade her father had received.

Seth focused on his food while the three talked. Seeing the distance between Lauren and her father made him realize he'd been lucky. He'd always been free to chart his own course in life. Even when he'd dropped out of school, his dad had been disappointed but understood that was Seth's decision to make.

"I understand from Adam that you're a rancher," Edmund said, finally acknowledging Seth.

"That's right."

"Seth graduated at the top of our high school class," Adam said. "Beat me out for valedictorian."

Lauren shifted sideways in her seat to face Seth. "You never told me that."

"Ancient history." Seth couldn't believe Adam had

even brought up the topic. "And definitely not a big deal."

"Still, you could have gone far," Adam said. "Of course you'd have had to leave Sweet River to realize that potential."

"You didn't pursue higher education?" From the horror in Edmund's voice, Seth surmised there could be no greater crime.

"Seth has a degree in biology," Lauren said before he could answer. "And three years postgrad in a veterinary program."

"Those programs are usually a four-year course of study," Edmund said.

"They are," Seth said. "I didn't complete the program."

"Why not?" Edmund demanded.

"The decision was based on personal issues," Seth said.

"Seth has a daughter," Adam volunteered. "She's seven or eight."

"Dani's seven," Lauren said.

"Ah, you have a child." Edmund shook his head. "The death knell of most careers."

"I wouldn't trade my daughter for any degree." Seth spoke slowly and deliberately so there could be no mistaking his meaning. "I'm sure you understand."

"I was older than you are now when Lauren was born." Edmund sounded affronted that Seth would even compare their situations. "Both Margaret and I were well established in our careers. Even so, Lauren's birth had an impact."

Seth opened his mouth to ask Edmund if it was worth it, but shut it without speaking. After listening to Lauren's father all evening, he wasn't sure the response he'd get would be a positive one.

"What my father is trying to say is it's not a choice he'd have made." Lauren placed her fork on her plate.

"Don't put words in my mouth, Lauren."

"I'm only speaking the truth. You've told me since I was a little girl that you never wanted me. You said as much tonight."

"I admit that when your mother found out she was pregnant, I had reservations." Edmund spoke as if he was discussing a mathematical equation rather than his daughter. "And a prudent person considers *all* options. But we're proud of you and the direction your life is taking."

Seth found it interesting that Edmund felt it worth considering all options when faced with an unwanted pregnancy, but not when it came to his daughter's career preferences.

"Thank goodness she didn't go the hausfrau route, eh, Edmund?" Adam joked.

"A daughter of mine would never settle for such a pedestrian lifestyle," Edmund said with a dismissive wave. "If she did…she wouldn't be my daughter."

Lauren spent the next three days trying to put the dinner with her father out of her mind. Only once during the disastrous evening had Edmund shown any real interest in her, and that was when he'd been extolling the virtues of the position he'd handpicked for her. Otherwise he'd mostly ignored her.

Thank goodness Seth had offered to join them. With the handsome cowboy by her side, her father's behavior hadn't hurt as it usually did. Lauren's only regret was that she hadn't told Seth how much his support had meant. She'd thought she'd do it over breakfast, but early the next morning he'd left to attend a cattleman's convention.

The rancher who was originally supposed to speak had come down with laryngitis and Seth had been asked to fill in. Before he agreed, Seth had asked Lauren if she felt comfortable handling Dani on her own. She assured him she'd be fine. The little girl had made a quicker-than-expected recovery and was now walking easily on her rocker-boot. Actually it wouldn't be long until she was independent again. That knowledge made Lauren determined to savor every minute of their remaining time together.

This love of children was something new Lauren had discovered about herself. She'd never thought much about kids. Before her stint as Dani's nanny, she'd have said she wasn't sure she wanted children. Or marriage. But her time with the Anderssen family had profoundly changed her.

Right now her favorite seven-year-old was in the family room reading while Lauren and Kim Sizemore sat at the kitchen table lingering over cups of tea. Kim's phone message this morning requesting a counseling session had been as unexpected as Seth's call to go out of town. With Seth gone and only her and Dani's schedule to work around, Lauren had called the accountant back and told her to come right over.

The session had ended but Lauren sensed something still preyed on the woman's mind.

Kim broke off a piece of shortbread cookie. "I heard Seth is coming home today."

"He should be here by suppertime." Lauren couldn't stop the smile that rose to her lips.

Kim took a sip of tea and gazed at Lauren over the rim of the cup. "Loretta Barbee mentioned he was out of town. How long has he been gone?"

"He left the day before yesterday." The fifty-five hours he'd been gone so far—not that she was counting—had felt like an eternity. How insane was that?

When Anna and Stacie had talked about missing their husbands, Lauren had been skeptical. So they were gone for a few days. Big deal. Her mother didn't see her father for months at a time. Missing him had never been an issue.

But Lauren missed Seth with a longing bordering on the ridiculous. She'd tried to make sense of it but hadn't been able to come up with a logical explanation. Unless perhaps she missed him simply because they'd spent so much time together recently. She'd gotten used to talking to him, to having him around. Yes, that must be it. Seth was like a familiar slipper, a favorite robe, a relaxing cup of cocoa.

A cup of cocoa?

Hmm…no. The sexy cowboy might be like a shot of whiskey but never warm milk. Lauren stifled a smile and took a sip of tea.

"I wish I had someone waiting for me at home," Kim said with a sigh.

"I'm just Seth's friend," Lauren reminded the woman, shrugging aside the sadness that welled inside her at the knowledge she would never be more. "He comes home to Dani, not to me."

"Oh." An odd look of disappointment crossed Kim's

face. "It's just that you're together all the time. I assumed you were a couple."

Lauren shook her head. Sometimes she found herself thinking of them as a couple and *she* knew better.

"Is that because of you and Adam?" Kim asked. "I know you've gone to dinner with him several times." An easy smile remained on her lips while her fingers tore a paper napkin into little strips. "Are you two dating?"

Lauren dropped her cup to the saucer with a clatter. She couldn't believe this ridiculous rumor was still floating around Sweet River. "Adam is a colleague of my father's," she said in a firm tone, hoping to end this nonsense once and for all. "That's our *only* connection."

"Good." Kim's cheeks turned bright pink. "I mean, that's good to know."

"You like Adam." Lauren kept any judgment from her voice but inside she worried. From what he'd said, Adam was only in Sweet River to settle his father's estate. Once he finished his business here, he would return to Rhode Island and Kim would be left behind.

"I told myself not to get emotionally involved." Kim glanced down at the tattered napkin and crumpled the paper into a ball. "But I discovered feelings aren't turned on and off that easily."

"I hear you." It was the same for Lauren. She'd tried to bury her feelings for Seth, knowing there could be no future with him. But it didn't matter. She loved him.

She. Loved. Seth.

Her heart stopped, then rose to her throat. All the things she'd been telling herself were true. She liked

Seth. Respected Seth. Had fun with Seth. But some-where along the way she'd also fallen in love with him.

Instead of joy, the thought brought only despair. For her and Seth, there could be no happily-ever-after.

Kim dropped a sugar cube into her cup. "Where will you go once you leave here?"

"Back to Denver for a short time, then I'll be moving to Virginia." Lauren tried to inject some enthusiasm into her voice. After all, as her father said, it was a solid opportunity. "I'm planning to accept a position on the faculty of King's College once I complete my degree."

"That's exciting." Kim finished the last of her tea. "Will you be doing counseling on the side or through the college?"

"Unfortunately neither." Lauren ignored the ping in her heart. "At least not initially."

"That's a shame." Kim pushed back her chair and stood. "You're a fabulous therapist. Easy to talk to and very helpful."

Lauren didn't know how helpful she'd been. Kim's reason for the session—a conflict with a fellow coworker—had been so trivial it had almost seemed, well, contrived.

"Thanks, Kim. I appreciate the kind words." Lauren rose and walked the accountant to the front door.

Kim paused at the front steps of the porch and turned to face Lauren. "Adam left a message on my cell this morning. He asked me to go to the movies and then to dinner."

Ah, today's visit finally made sense.

Lauren cocked her head. "What did you tell him?"

"Nothing yet. But I'm going to call him back and say

yes. I think we're a good match." A tiny smile hovered on the edges of Kim's lips. "Just like the survey indicated."

Lauren thought about the survey *she'd* completed. Even if she and Seth matched, it wouldn't make a difference. "You'll have to let me know how it goes."

"Maybe I'll be inviting you to a wedding someday," Kim said with a laugh.

Lauren merely smiled. It hardly seemed possible, but then again, stranger things had happened.

They talked for a few more minutes before Kim got into her car and Lauren headed inside. She paused in the foyer and glanced at the side table, her gaze settling on a manila envelope Anna had delivered yesterday. The envelope with the survey results. No, not just *the* survey results, *her* survey results. She'd done the analysis, but had chickened out and had Anna do the number matching.

Lauren picked up the envelope, weighing it in her hands.

Sometimes it seemed as if she'd spent her entire life wanting what she couldn't have. She'd always known she wasn't a priority in her father's life, but at least she thought he loved her. A couple nights ago it had been made clear that he only wanted her in his life if she fit into a nice, tidy slot. And she could finally admit that with the previous men in her life, she'd settled for less than she deserved by telling herself that's all she wanted.

Lying to herself had become a pattern. She'd told herself she didn't need or want more than she'd been given. But she did. She wanted a man who would love her mind as much as he loved her body. She wanted a man who would be her best friend. She wanted a man willing and able to commit to her one hundred percent.

If only Seth were free to love me. If only—

She slammed the door shut on the pointless wishing. Wishing things were different didn't change the reality. There was no room in Seth's life for her. Whether they matched or not was a moot point.

Lauren strolled over to the nearest wastebasket and dropped in the envelope.

Chapter Seventeen

Lauren stood on the porch and breathed in the fresh Montana air. For mid-January, a sunny day in the upper-fifties was practically balmy. She'd done a few chores after Kim had left. Then, feeling restless, had taken a stroll around the yard. She'd asked Dani if she wanted to come outside, but Dani had moved from her homework to teaching Bailey some special "super-duper" trick as a welcome-home surprise for Seth.

Lifting her face to the sun, Lauren reveled in the warmth against her cheeks. She wasn't sure how long she stood there. Only that the sound of an engine snapped her to attention.

A bright red pickup rounded the curve in the driveway, and Lauren's heart gave a leap. She opened the front door. "Dani, Daddy's home."

"Don't let him come inside," Dani called back, her voice filled with panic. "Bailey's not cooperating."

"I'll stall," Lauren promised. She shut the door and returned to the front rail, trying to still the excitement rising inside her.

The truck pulled to a stop and Seth stepped out. He wore her favorite shirt—the one Anna had given him for his birthday. The one that made his eyes look as blue as the ocean.

Lauren was seized with the sudden urge to run to him, like a heroine from an old-time movie when her husband comes home from war. But he wasn't her husband. He wasn't even her boyfriend. Still, he was home and she couldn't stop joy from sluicing through her veins.

Seth ambled up the walk, the sun highlighting the gold in his hair, those gorgeous eyes focused directly on her. He paused at the bottom of the steps. "Hello, Lauren."

Her cheeks heated under the intensity of his gaze. "Hello, Seth."

Keeping his gaze firmly on her face, he climbed the steps. In seconds he stood an arm's length away, close enough to touch but not touching. "Where's Dani?"

"Your little dog trainer is inside showing Bailey a new trick. But shh." She touched a finger to her lips. "It's a surprise."

He took a step closer, his gaze lingering on her lips. "Discretion is my middle name."

The air sizzled with electricity. Her knees turned to jelly and she tightened her fingers around the porch rail for support.

"I missed you," he murmured. "God, how I missed you."

The words seemed to come out of nowhere. For a second she wondered if she'd only imagined them. Until she saw the look in his eyes.

"I missed you, too." The admission flowed from her heart. In a matter of days she'd be gone. Nothing was going to change that outcome. But for these few fleeting moments she would be honest. With him. With herself. "I felt as if part of me was missing. I know it sounds silly…"

"Not silly at all," he said. "I couldn't wait to get back here. As soon as I finished, I jumped in the truck and headed home."

Lauren's heart skipped a beat. She gestured to the porch swing. "Do you have time to sit for a few minutes? Dani is working with Bailey on a new trick. She wants him to have it mastered before you come inside."

"Actually I was hoping we'd have some time alone." He rocked back on his heels and grinned at her questioning look. "I have something for you. It's in the truck."

"For me?" Lauren swallowed against the sudden lump in her throat. She couldn't remember ever getting a gift for no reason.

"Just a little something I saw in a store and thought you'd like," he said.

"Well, go get it." She gave him a little push. "The suspense is killing me."

Lauren shifted from one foot to the other, watching his every step. When he reached into the truck and pulled out a yellow plastic bag, she narrowed her gaze. What kind of gift came in a grocery bag?

Seth shoved the bag under his arm like it was a football and headed up the walk.

"It's a belated Christmas present," he said when he reached the porch.

"You already gave me a Christmas gift." Lauren held up her arm, the silver bracelet glinting in the sun. "I love it."

"I think you'll love this, too," he said. "At least I hope you do."

"I'm sure I will." Lauren reached for the bag but he tucked it behind his back, out of reach.

"Sit on the swing," he said. "Then close your eyes."

"If you're planning on putting on the Santa suit for this, I'm telling you right now, it's not necessary."

He laughed and she laughed along with him as they walked to the swing, his hand nearly, but not quite touching hers. The breeze ruffled his hair and carried the scent of his cologne to her. She inhaled deeply, reveling in this perfect moment in time, committing it to memory.

Lauren took a seat on the swing and promptly held out her hand. "Merry belated Christmas to me."

A smile tugged at the corners of Seth's lips. "Eyes shut first."

Lauren did as he'd requested, but as soon as he placed the bag in her hands, her lids popped open.

Seth settled himself beside her, an expectant look on his face.

Lauren took a deep breath and reached inside. Even if she didn't like it—

Her heart stopped. With a trembling hand, Lauren

gently pulled the doll the rest of the way from the bag. She looked at him in disbelief. "It's a Cabbage Patch Kid."

The doll had bright red hair pulled into two pigtails. Her dress was cornflower blue with buttercup-yellow flowers, and she had white shoes and yellow socks. Lauren let her gaze linger. This was the Cabbage Patch Kid of her childhood dreams.

"Her name is Lottie Rose," Seth volunteered.

"You remembered." Lauren clutched the doll close. "Where did you find her?"

"In an antique shop not far from the hotel where we were meeting," he said. "I saw her in the window and thought of you."

"I *love* her." Lauren fingered the yarnlike hair. A couple of tears slipped down her cheeks. The fact that Seth had gone out of his way to do something just because it would make her happy made the gift even more special. "I don't know what I've done to deserve this, but thank you."

"You deserve to be spoiled and pampered and given gifts." Seth's voice turned husky. "I hope you find someone special in Virginia, someone who'll make you as happy as you've made Dani and me."

Virginia. Was it only a coincidence that the sun— which had been shining hot and bright—chose this moment to disappear behind the clouds?

"I've loved every minute of my time here." Lauren tightened her hold on the doll. "Thank you for everything, Seth. For opening your home to me, for letting me be a part of your family these past few weeks…and for Lottie."

She clutched the doll tightly against her chest, suddenly overcome with emotion.

He frowned. "That sounds an awful lot like good-bye."

"Dani gets her arm cast off Monday." The words came out faint and faraway. Lauren cleared her throat and tried again. "Depending on the X-rays, the boot cast could be removed by the end of the week."

"Time has gone fast." Unexpectedly Seth grasped her hand, holding it tight. "I wish I could make it stand still."

"Not a possibility," Lauren said lightly, ignoring the ache in her heart. "But there is something I want to say before I go. Actually two things."

Seth laced his fingers loosely through hers. "What's on your mind?"

"I want to thank you for going with me to dinner the other night. Your support really meant a lot."

"Anytime," he said, his gaze watchful. "What was the second?"

"I want you to be happy."

"I want the same for you." His thumb began to caress the center of her palm and forming a coherent thought became increasingly difficult.

"No, you don't understand. I want you to find a way to make your dreams of becoming a veterinarian come true," Lauren explained. "Promise me you'll see if there's any way you can finish the program."

The fact that Seth's fingers remained twined with hers and he didn't pull away gave her courage to continue.

"You have so much talent, so much compassion, so

much love…for animals." Her tongue stumbled for a second. "I don't want to see you waste it."

Thankfully he didn't appear to take offense. Instead his brows pulled together and a thoughtful look crossed his face.

"I've thought about going back many times over the past three years," Seth admitted. He shifted his position so he faced her. "But I'll look at the logistics again *if* you promise you'll do the same."

"Look at becoming a veterinarian?"

Seth laughed and the sun broke through the clouds. "No, I want you to look at what makes *you* happy. Maybe it's teaching. Maybe it's research. Maybe it's counseling. But before you embark on a new career, make sure you're following your passion, or as Stacie would say, your bliss. You're an amazing woman, Lauren. You deserve a wonderful life."

Lauren's heart rose to her throat. "Sounds like we both want the best for each other."

He reached up and—for a second—cupped her face with his hand. "That's how it is when you lo— care for someone."

In that moment, under the bright Montana sun, Lauren realized Seth wasn't just the man she loved, he was her soul mate.

She was seized with the sudden urge to pull him close, to run her fingers through his hair, to feel the muscles in his back tighten beneath her fingers. To hold him tight and never let go.

But she didn't act on the impulse. Because she knew her only choice was to walk away. Seth's integrity was as much a part of him as his cowboy boots and quick smile. And she couldn't ask him to abandon the promise he'd made to his dying wife, not even for her.

Two days later Lauren moved back into the house Anna had inherited from her grandma. Seth hated to see her go. She was only going to be in Sweet River one more week anyway and in his mind it made no sense for her to move twice. But she insisted. Though she'd done her best to prepare his daughter, the day Lauren moved out, Dani cried. Seth understood. He felt as if someone had reached inside his chest and torn out his heart.

The last thing Lauren had done had been to stick out her hand. But instead of a polite handshake he'd pulled her into his arms and held her with a fierceness that surprised them both. By the time he took a step back her eyes—and his—were suspiciously moist.

Today though, he was going to do his best not to think of Lauren. This was "Jan's Day." Every year since her passing, he and Dani celebrated her birthday by doing things they'd once done as a family.

He'd gotten the idea when he'd heard a mother on the radio talking about her little boy, David, who'd passed away. Once a year on his birthday, his family celebrated "David's Day." It was their way of keeping his memory alive and celebrating his life.

"Dani," Seth called out. "Breakfast is ready."

His daughter had gotten the cast off her arm yesterday. He'd expected her to be bouncing off the walls with joy, but she'd been uncharacteristically silent. He knew she missed Lauren. Heck, he missed her, too.

He flipped the waffle onto a platter with extra force

and split it onto two plates. He added cherry topping and whipped cream just as Dani walked into the room, the boot cast barely slowing her down. Lauren had been right. Physically, Dani didn't need her anymore. Emotionally, however, was another story.

Seth forced a smile and poured two glasses of orange juice. "I hope you're hungry."

Dani took a seat at the table, but instead of digging in, she simply gazed down at the golden-brown waffle.

Seth sat opposite her. "Remember how Mommy used to make waffles for us every Sunday before church?"

Dani nodded and picked up her folk. "I miss Mommy."

"I know you do, princess," Seth said automatically. But the minute the words left his mouth he realized the pain that had always accompanied thoughts of Jan had disappeared.

For a second he felt a twinge of guilt. Until he remembered his grandmother promising him during the depth of his grief that this day would come. She'd told him that when he could enjoy the memories of the life he'd shared with Jan without his heart aching, that was when he'd know he was ready to move on with his life.

"Maybe Miss Lauren can come to the penny pond with us today." The hopeful gleam in the little girl's eyes tore at Seth's heartstrings.

"I don't think so," Seth said gently. "But you and me, we'll have a good time. I have a whole pocketful of pennies. You can make lots and lots of wishes."

Years ago, someone had supposedly thrown a penny

into a particular pond near town and made a wish. When the wish had come true, the pond achieved local lore status.

"I only need one penny," Dani said.

"You only have one wish?" Seth teased.

"Yep." Dani smeared the cherry topping over the top of her waffle and added a big blob of whipped cream.

"What's the wish?" Seth asked, suddenly curious.

Dani smiled. "If I tell you, it won't come true."

"Duh, I knew that." Seth smacked himself on the side of his head with the flat of his palm, the exaggerated gesture bringing giggles from his daughter.

But only a moment later, Dani's little face grew serious. "Before Mommy died, she told me a secret."

Seth placed his fork on the table. "What was the secret?"

Dani's mouth closed over a big bite of waffle. She chewed for several seconds then took a sip of juice. "Mommy told me that even though I was sad because she was leaving me, I'd be happy again. That you would make sure we were happy."

While it definitely sounded like something Jan would have said, Seth wasn't sure the comment qualified as a secret. Surely there had to be more. "What else did she say?"

Dani shrugged and dropped her gaze to the plate. "Nothing."

"You can tell me," Seth said as persuasively as he could. "You know there isn't anything you can't tell me."

"Mommy didn't say anything else. I just didn't think it was true." Dani whispered the words. "But then you brought Miss Lauren home. It was like Mommy said, we were all happy. But—"

"But what?"

"You let her leave." Dani lifted her gaze and the look in her eyes broke his heart. "Why did you do that, Daddy? Why did you let her leave?"

Seth hoped the walk to the park on Main Street would clear his head. It wasn't even noon and he was already drained. After trying to answer Dani's questions in a way she could understand, they'd headed to the penny pond where Dani had insisted on throwing one—and only one—penny into the water.

Now she was eating a catered lunch at Sew-fisticated with Anna and several women who'd been Jan's childhood friends. That gave him an hour of thinking time.

He'd just reached the gate to the town park when Mitch pulled his 4x4 to the curb with Josh in the passenger seat.

Seth walked over to them. "What's up?"

"Anna's hosting some luncheon at the shop." Mitch jerked a thumb in Josh's direction. "Stacie's helping Lauren pack."

"You're a fool if you let her leave," a voice called out from the sidewalk.

An eerie sense of déjà vu washed over him. Seth forced a smile and turned. Loretta Barbee—who must have either been already in the park or lurking behind the large evergreen—stood in front of the gate.

"Mrs. Barbee," he said. "Good afternoon."

"I'm disappointed in you, Seth Anderssen," she said, apparently deciding to forgo a greeting and get right to the point. "I know what's been going on between you and Lauren Van Meveren. I'm shocked that you—"

"Hold your horses." Seth raised a hand, his voice as tight as a crossbow. "Nothing improper occurred between Lauren and me."

"I'm not saying it did. But you are in love with her," Loretta said. "That's as plain as the nose on my face. What I and the rest of this town can't figure out is why you're letting her leave."

"It's complicated," Seth muttered, wondering why he bothered saying anything. It wasn't like any of this was her business.

"It's only as complicated as you make it." The woman's gaze shifted over Seth's shoulder, and her expression brightened. She smiled and waved. "Cassie. Wait a second. We need to talk."

Keeping the smile firmly on her face, the pastor's wife lowered her voice to a confidential whisper. "Alex Darst is going to propose. Cassie will say yes. Then they'll put a bid on your grandma Borghild's house. But remember, you didn't hear the news from me."

She hurried off without a backward glance.

Sounds of laughter erupted from the truck.

Seth scowled and turned back to his friends. "Yeah, she's a barrel of laughs."

Josh's smile faded. "She's right about one thing. Lauren *is* leaving. Stacie and Anna are taking her to the airport tomorrow. If you don't do something quickly, she'll be gone."

Seth could have brought up the vow he'd made to Jan, but after his conversation with Dani this morning, he'd come to a realization. The promise his wife had demanded had simply been Jan's way of trying to ensure her daughter's happiness.

Even though Mitch had said the promise made it appear Jan hadn't trusted him, he knew she had. What she'd said to Dani had sounded like the woman he'd married, the woman who all her life had trusted him to do the right thing. The woman who'd promised Dani he'd do what was necessary for them to have happy lives. That woman would have never tied his hands.

But if he really believed that, why wasn't he on Lauren's doorstep right now?

"She's at your grandma Borghild's house now," Josh said. "I can call Stacie, make up some excuse to get my wife out of there so you can have some time alone with Lauren."

Still, Seth hesitated. He loved Lauren. But this wasn't just about him. He wanted to do the right thing for her.

"Spit it out, Anderssen," Mitch taunted. "What's holding you back?"

"Lauren is the smartest woman I've ever known," Seth said. "She has a great future ahead of her. Is it fair to ask her to give it all up for me?"

"I don't think she'd be giving it *all* up for you," Mitch said with a wry smile. "She could have a good life in Sweet River."

"Let Lauren make the decision," Josh urged.

"He's right," Mitch echoed before Seth could respond. "Think about how hurt Anna was when you didn't initially invite us over for Christmas Eve. Not asking takes the choice away. What's fair about that?"

"Nothing." In fact, Seth realized that's what Lauren's

father had always done, or, rather, attempted to do. "If she doesn't want to stay, she'll have no trouble telling me no."

Mitch chuckled. "Glad to hear you're going in with a positive attitude."

Seth fixed his gaze on Josh. "Call Stacie. Say whatever you need to say to get her out of that house. Lauren and I have some serious talkin' to do."

Chapter Eighteen

Lauren dumped a pile of shoes on the bed and tried not to listen to what was obviously a private conversation. Based on the ring tone, she knew Stacie was talking to her husband. But instead of chattering a mile a minute, her friend was doing an awful lot of listening. Lauren couldn't wait to find out what was so fascinating.

Stacie slid the top of her phone shut, her cheeks a bright pink. "That was definitely interesting."

Pushing the shoes aside, Lauren plopped down on the bed. "What did he have to say?"

The pink darkened to a dusky rose. "He wants us to, uh, get together. Have some fun of the bedroom variety. He said he was coming to get me and didn't even give me a chance to say yes or no."

"You're newlyweds. I'm sure he knows you're interested." Lauren fought back a pang of envy. "My only question is, why aren't you waiting at the door?"

Stacie glanced around the bedroom cluttered with suitcases and clothes and shoes. "I promised to help you pack."

"There's still tonight. *If* you're not too worn out," Lauren teased. When Stacie still hesitated, Lauren rose to her feet, grabbed her friend's arm and pushed her toward the door. "Go. If I had a husband who called me for a little afternoon delight, you can bet I wouldn't be standing here talking to my girlfriend."

Stacie gave Lauren a quick hug. "I'll be back soon."

"Take your time," Lauren said. "I'm not going anywhere."

Today was a packing-and-tying-up-loose-ends day. Tomorrow she'd say her final goodbyes and hop a plane to Denver. Her friends still thought she'd be moving to Virginia, but after her talk with Seth, she'd done some serious thinking.

Just this morning she'd made her decision. Though King's College was a well-respected institution, going there didn't feel right. So she'd followed her gut and declined the offer.

After she received her PhD from the University of Denver, Lauren would decide where *she* wanted to settle. Not where her father thought was best, but a place that would feed her soul as well as allow her to best utilize all her skills.

Being in Sweet River had made her realize that for her, "success" wasn't tenure at an Ivy League college or a list of publications in a scholarly journal. It was doing what she loved—teaching and counseling—while surrounded by people she loved.

In that respect, Sweet River would be a perfect place to settle. Her friends were here. She'd already started to build a practice. And with the boom in Internet educational offerings, there might even be the possibility of teaching some online courses.

There was only one problem—Seth. While it was going to be hard to move away, Lauren knew it would be harder to stay. Seeing him, wanting him and knowing he could never be hers would be pure torture.

No, she had to leave. After she received her PhD she would look for another small town, one where she could feel part of a community. Where she could make friends and start to build a life. A life without Seth and Dani.

Lauren was still lost in thought when she heard a light tapping followed by the front door creaking open. She blinked back the tears and hurried down the stairs, ready to set her friend straight. Stacie's priority right now should be Josh. She could do her own packing, thank you very much.

She turned the corner with the words poised on her lips and skidded to a stop. "Seth. What are you doing here?"

Her gaze lingered on his face. On the strong masculine features. On the laugh lines and the worry lines. On the eyes that reflected honesty and integrity. A deep sorrow rose inside her. She couldn't imagine ever loving another man as much as she loved him.

"You can't leave me," he said.

The desperation and pain in his voice told her she

wasn't the only one suffering. The knowledge gave her little solace. She didn't want Seth or Dani to hurt because of her.

Not trusting herself to speak, she just shrugged.

He took a step closer. "I love you."

The sweet words were a balm to her aching heart. She would try to remember this moment on cold winter nights when she was alone and missing him.

He stared, an expectant look on his face.

"I love you, too," she admitted.

"Thank you, God." He moved close and pulled her to him. "Don't leave, Lauren. Stay with me. Please."

Lauren let herself return his hug, but only for a moment. Then she stepped back, untangling herself from his arms. "I can't, Seth. You know that as well as I do."

"I don't know any such thing," he said with a fierceness that took her breath away. "We belong together. I love you. You love me."

"That fact changes nothing." He was too honorable a man to break his promise, and she loved him too much to ask. "I can't stay and just be your friend."

"Who said anything about friends?" He grabbed her hands, and when she tried to pull away, his grip tightened. "I love you, Lauren. More than I thought possible. I want to spend the rest of my life with you, loving you, cherishing you, making you happy. I want—"

"Stop." Lauren jerked back her hands, thankful the rising anger kept her tears at bay. "Why are you doing this? You have to know how much it hurts to think of being apart from you and Dani. But you made a vow to Jan. Us being together isn't an option."

"But—"

"I think it's best if you leave."

His feet remained firmly planted and a look she couldn't quite decipher filled her eyes. "Please, Lauren. Give me five minutes. That's all I'm asking."

The pleading in his voice was nearly her undoing. She cleared her throat and nodded. "Five minutes."

Lauren led him to the parlor and perched on the edge of the sofa, expecting him to settle himself in the chair. Instead, he dropped beside her. With a resigned sigh she shifted to face him, inhaling the tantalizing scent of his cologne, reminding herself that what wouldn't kill her would make her stronger.

"This is so important…." Seth blew out a breath and raked a hand through his hair. "I'm not as good with words as you are, so please bear with me."

His voice shook. Seth was the most confident guy she knew. To see him so unsure and stressed tugged at her heartstrings.

"It's okay," she said in a soft whisper. "Take all the time you need."

Unexpectedly he captured her hand. "I can't be this close and not touch you."

Her breath hitched in her throat. The feel of his calloused hand against hers was pure heaven. The hell was in knowing this was the last time she'd feel his touch. She wanted to wrap her arms around his broad shoulders and never let go. But forever wasn't an option for them. Had never been an option. She squeezed his hand and offered an encouraging smile anyway.

"When Jan asked for my promise not to marry again until Dani was out of high school, it took me by surprise. While I knew her mother had remarried when she was a child and that Jan and her stepfather had never gotten along, I hadn't realized how deeply she'd been scarred. Jan loved Dani so much. She couldn't bear to think of her daughter one day being in that same situation."

Lauren had known motherly love existed, but had never experienced what a driving force it could be until she'd spent time with Dani. Her heart went out to Jan. How frightening it must have been for her, knowing she was going to die and leave her precious child behind. "She wanted Dani to always feel special and loved."

Seth nodded. "I know Jan trusted me to take care of Dani. She's always trusted me." His fingers tightened around Lauren's hand. "That's why the more I thought about it, the more I realized I'd been so focused on the promise itself, I hadn't considered the intent of the vow."

Lauren was now thoroughly confused. "I'm not sure I understand."

"Jan wanted me to be happy. She wanted Dani to be happy. From that hospital bed, it must have seemed the only way to ensure our happiness was for me to remain single. But she couldn't have known about you. She couldn't have known that there was someone out there who'd one day walk into our lives and bring such joy and happiness to both of us."

He jerked to his feet, strode to the mantel, then turned. "If she had, I know from the deepest part of my being, she wouldn't want that promise to keep you from us. Because the only thing she ever wanted was for Dani and me to be happy. We've found that happiness with you. We both love you, Lauren."

The tears that had begun filling Lauren's eyes slipped down her cheeks. She brushed them away with the backs of her hands. While she was afraid to hope for too much, her heart gave an excited leap. "Where do we go from here?"

"That depends." He resumed his seat and leaned forward, resting his elbows on his knees. "Once you finish your PhD you could go anywhere in the country. Heck, you already have a job—"

"I turned it down."

"What?"

"It was a career-building opportunity, but that's not what I want." Her voice trembled, then broke. She cleared her throat. "Tenure with an Ivy League college was my father's dream, not mine."

His eyes searched hers. "What is *your* dream, Lauren? If you could live anywhere in the world, do anything you wanted, what would you choose?"

He'd asked her that question before, back when she'd encouraged him to pursue *his* dream of being a vet. At that time she hadn't known what course she wanted her life to take. This time there was no doubt.

"I want to live in Sweet River, have a small counseling practice, perhaps teach some online courses. I want to be close to my friends." Lauren paused, praying she wasn't misreading his signals. She wanted a life with this man and with the little girl she loved as if she were her own. She took a deep breath and plunged ahead. "Most of all, I want to be with you. You and Dani are what I want. I love you both very, very much."

A smile bright enough to light the state of Montana flashed across his face. "I was hoping you'd say that."

Slipping from the sofa, Seth dropped to one knee and once again took her hand. "Lauren Van Meveren, will you marry me? Will you be my wife and Dani's mother?"

Lauren's heart pounded so hard she could hear the blood rushing in her ears. If she was dreaming, she never wanted to wake up.

"Yes," she said, then again more loudly in case he hadn't heard, "Yes. I'd be honored to be your wife… and Dani's mother."

Before she could take a breath, Seth was on his feet, wrapping his arms round her, holding her as if he'd never let her go. As his lips closed over hers, Lauren realized with a sense of wonder that just like Stacie and Anna, she'd found her true bliss…in the town of Sweet River, in the arms of the cowboy she loved.

Epilogue

One month later

The last quilting class of the evening might have concluded an hour ago, but Sew-fisticated still buzzed with activity. Stacie had supplied the appetizers and Cassie had uncorked a bottle of champagne left over from the holidays to complete the impromptu post–Valentine's Day party.

"Let me look at that ring, Mrs. Anderssen," Cassie said.

Lauren held up her left hand. The large emerald-cut diamond with the filigreed roses on the band sent flashes of light scattering. Seth had inherited the ring with the antique setting from his great-grandmother, shortly after Jan passed on. He'd offered to let her pick out a new one, a more modern one, but this ring had seen a lifetime of love and suited her just fine.

Two weeks after Seth had proposed they'd been married by Pastor Barbee in a small ceremony attended by family and friends. Adam and Kim had arrived together, looking very much a "couple." Lauren's parents had managed to fit the wedding into their busy schedules and had even gotten along for the brief time they'd been together. It had been a little tense at first, but when Edmund had started in about Lauren "ruining her life," Seth had made it clear he wasn't going to allow anything to mar Lauren's wedding day, and her father had shut up.

When Seth and Lauren had announced they'd be accepting Anna and Mitch's invitation to join them on their delayed honeymoon in the Caribbean in March— after Lauren defended her dissertation—Stacie and Josh had decided to go along, too. Dani kept asking when they were leaving. She and Bailey were staying with Cassie, and the little girl couldn't wait to play hide-and-seek in Grandma Borghild's big house on Main Street.

There'd been other changes, as well. Seth had contacted Central Montana State, and next fall he'd be resuming his veterinary studies. Though that meant the next year and a half would be extra busy, they both agreed the result would be worth it.

"That is such a gorgeous ring," Cassie gushed.

"Yours is beautiful, too." Lauren smiled. Alex Darst had proposed to Cassie on the same day she and Seth had gotten married. Their wedding was scheduled for the end of the month—just in time for the couple to close on Grandma Borghild's house.

"Loretta Barbee is taking credit for both weddings," Stacie said with a wry smile.

"Don't let Dani hear you say that." Anna lowered her voice, probably because the child was in the next room with her buddy Brandon, cutting out quilting squares. "She's convinced *she* brought her dad and Lauren together. Apparently she made a wish in the penny pond the same day Seth proposed to you."

"As far as I'm concerned, they can both take credit," Lauren said with a smile. She glanced toward the back room. "Remember the quilt Jan had started for Dani? Well, I talked to Seth and he thinks it's a great idea for Dani and me to finish it together."

"I'm so happy he approved," Anna said. "And don't worry that you've never quilted before. Stacie and Cassie and I will help you."

"That's right. Everyone working together is the Sweet River way," Stacie said. "Coming here was the smartest move the three of us could have made."

"You won't hear any argument from me," Lauren said.

"Did you ever think when you developed your survey that we'd all end up finding our perfect matches?" Stacie asked. "Your research project led me straight to Josh."

"And me back to Mitch," Anna said.

"We each found our perfect match." Cassie lifted a glass of champagne. "Thanks to your dissertation research."

Anna cast a pointed glance at Lauren. "And don't forget, you found Seth."

"Well, I found him," Lauren said. "But I'm not sure

we matched…on paper, that is. But regardless of what the results may have shown, my husband is definitely the man for me."

"I'm confused. You both completed surveys," Stacie said. "Don't you know if you matched?"

"Anna correlated the numbers," Lauren admitted. "But I threw out the results without looking at them."

"Were they in a manila envelope?" Anna asked.

Lauren nodded.

"Mitch brought the packet home," Anna said. "You'd put my name on the front when you'd originally given it to me. Seth found it in the trash and returned it to Mitch, thinking it was mine."

Lauren's heart skipped a beat. "You have the packet?"

Anna nodded. "It's in the back room. I've been meaning to give it to you, but we were so busy with your wedding that I forgot. I'm sorry."

"It's not important." Lauren waved the champagne flute. "I have the man I love. That's all that matters."

"You may not be curious, but I sure am." Anna popped out of her chair and disappeared into the back room, returning moments later with the envelope.

She handed it to Lauren just as the shop door jingled and Seth walked in.

Love welled up inside Lauren, the way it always did at the sight of the handsome rancher. A soft smile curled her lips. It was still hard to believe he was hers.

He crossed the room quickly and planted a lingering kiss on her lips. "Ready to go? I'd like to get home."

Her heart fluttered at the seductive expression in his eyes. She knew exactly what he had planned once Dani was in bed. It was the same thing she had in mind. Married life had turned out even better than she'd imagined, both in and out of the bedroom. Seth had been right. Love and sexual intimacy were a potent combination.

"Open the packet before you leave," Anna urged.

Seth cocked an eyebrow. "Packet?"

"She'll explain later," Anna said.

"This is so exciting." Stacie leaned forward, resting her arms on the table.

Lauren glanced at their expectant gazes. It appeared she had no choice. She unfastened the top of the envelope and pulled out the sheet, telling herself it didn't matter what the survey results showed. Seth was the love of her life. No piece of paper was going to convince her otherwise.

Still, she held her breath as she searched the form, recognizing his number…right next to hers. She lifted her eyes. "We're a perfect match."

One corner of his mouth turned up in a smile. "You can say that again."

A wave of love washed over her, nearly drowning her in its wake.

"Daddy, Daddy." Dani came running out of the back room with Lottie Rose in her arms. The Cabbage Patch Kid had been Lauren's wedding present to her new daughter. Dani glanced around the room at all the women staring at Lauren with big smiles on their faces. "What's wrong?"

"Nothing's wrong," Anna said. "Lauren's survey confirmed she and your daddy were meant to be best friends."

Dani turned to Lauren, confusion blanketing her face. "I thought you and me were bestest friends."

Seth turned to his daughter and winked. "That's the great thing about friends," he said. "You can never have too many."

The child thought for a moment, then nodded. "Just like presents. You can never have too many presents."

Anna laughed and waved her hand. "I'll second that."

"Let me see your Cabbage Patch Kid, Dani," Stacie said. "I don't think Lottie and I have been introduced."

As the child proudly showed off her doll, Seth turned to Lauren. "You didn't have to give it to her," he said in a low voice. "It was your gift."

"I wanted her to have it." Lauren wrapped her arms around his neck, her heart overflowing with love. She put her lips to his ear. "Besides, I have you. And, cowboy, you're the bestest Christmas present ever."

* * * * *

*Celebrate 60 years of pure reading pleasure
with Harlequin®!
Just in time for the holidays,
Silhouette Special Edition® is proud to present
New York Times bestselling author
Kathleen Eagle's
ONE COWBOY, ONE CHRISTMAS.*

Rodeo rider Zach Beaudry was a travelin' man—
until he broke down in middle-of-nowhere South
Dakota during a deep freeze. That's when an
angel came to his rescue....

"Don't die on me. Come on, Zel. You know how much I love you, girl. You're all I've got. Don't do this to me here. Not *now*."

But Zelda had quit on him, and Zach Beaudry had no one to blame but himself. He'd taken his sweet time hitting the road, and then miscalculated a shortcut. For all he knew he was a hundred miles from gas. But even if they were sitting next to a pump, the ten dollars he had in his pocket wouldn't get him out of South Dakota, which was not where he wanted to be right now. Not even his beloved pickup truck, Zelda, could get him much of anywhere on fumes. He was sitting out in the cold in the middle of nowhere. And getting colder.

He shifted the pickup into Neutral and pulled hard

on the steering wheel, using the downhill slope to get her off the blacktop and into the roadside grass, where she shuddered to a standstill. He stroked the padded dash. "You'll be safe here."

But Zach would not. It was getting dark, and it was already too damn cold for his cowboy ass. Zach's battered body was a barometer, and he was feeling South Dakota, big-time. He'd have given his right arm to be climbing into a hotel hot tub instead of a brutal blast of north wind. The right was his free arm anyway. Damn thing had lost altitude, touched some part of the bull and caused him a scoreless ride last time out.

It wasn't scoring him a ride this night, either. A carload of teenagers whizzed by, topping off the insult by laying on the horn as they passed him. It was at least twenty minutes before another vehicle came along. He stepped out and waved both arms this time, damn near getting himself killed. Whatever happened to *do unto others?* In places like this, decent people didn't leave each other stranded in the cold.

His face was feeling stiff, and he figured he'd better start walking before his toes went numb. He struck out for a distant yard light, the only sign of human habitation in sight. He couldn't tell how distant, but he knew he'd be hurting by the time he got there, and he was counting on some kindly old man to be answering the door. No shame among the lame.

It wasn't like Zach was fresh off the operating table—it had been a few months since his last round of repairs—but he hadn't given himself enough time. He'd lopped a couple of weeks off the near end of the doc's estimated recovery time, rigged up a brace, done some heavy-duty taping and climbed onto another bull. Hung in there for five seconds—four seconds past feeling the pop in his hip and three seconds short of the buzzer.

He could still feel the pain shooting down his leg with every step. Only, this time he had to pick the damn thing up, swing it forward and drop it down again on his own.

Pride be damned, he just hoped *somebody* would be answering the door at the end of the road. The light in the front window was a good sign.

The four steps to the covered porch might as well have been four hundred, and he was looking to climb them with a lead weight chained to his left leg. His eyes were just as screwed up as his hip. Big black spots danced around with tiny red flashers, and he couldn't tell what was real and what wasn't. He stumbled over some shrubbery, steadied himself on the porch railing and peered between vertical slats.

There in the front window stood a spruce tree with a silver star affixed to the top. Zach was pretty sure the red sparks were all in his head, but the white lights twinkling by the hundreds throughout the huge tree, those were real. He wasn't too sure about the woman hanging the shiny balls. Most of her hair was caught up on her head and fastened in a curly clump, but the light captured by the escaped bits crowned her with a golden halo. Her face was a soft shadow, her body a willowy silhouette beneath a long white gown. If this was where the mind ran off to when cold started shutting down the rest of the body, then Zach's final worldly thought was, *This ain't such a bad way to go.*

If she would just turn to the window, he could die looking into the eyes of a Christmas angel.

* * * * *

Could this woman from Zach's past get the lonesome cowboy to come in from the cold...for good?

Look for
ONE COWBOY, ONE CHRISTMAS
by Kathleen Eagle.
Available December 2009
from Silhouette Special Edition®.

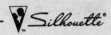

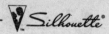

SPECIAL EDITION

**FROM *NEW YORK TIMES* AND *USA TODAY*
BESTSELLING AUTHOR**

KATHLEEN EAGLE

ONE COWBOY,
One Christmas

When bull rider Zach Beaudry appeared
out of thin air on Ann Drexler's ranch,
she thought she was seeing a ghost of
Christmas past. And though Zach had
no memory of their night of passion years
ago, they were about to share a future
he would never forget.

*Available December 2009
wherever books are sold.*

SSE65493

REQUEST YOUR FREE BOOKS!

2 FREE NOVELS PLUS 2 FREE GIFTS!

Silhouette®

SPECIAL EDITION®

Life, Love and Family!

SSE09R

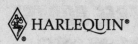

HARLEQUIN®

American ★ Romance®

A Cowboy Christmas
MARIN THOMAS

2 stories in 1!

The holidays are a rough time for widower
Logan Taylor and single dad Fletcher McFadden—
neither hunky cowboy has been lucky in love.
But Christmas is the season of miracles! Logan
meets his match in "A Christmas Baby," while
Fletcher gets a second chance at love in "Marry
Me, Cowboy." This year both cowboys are on
Santa's Nice list!

*Available December
wherever books are sold.*

"LOVE, HOME & HAPPINESS"

www.eHarlequin.com

HAR75292

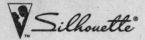

#2011 ONE COWBOY, ONE CHRISTMAS—Kathleen Eagle

When bull rider Zach Beaudry appeared out of thin air on Ann Drexler's ranch, she thought she was seeing a ghost of Christmas past. And though Zach had no memory of their night of passion years ago, they were about to share a future he would never forget.

#2012 CHRISTMAS AT BRAVO RIDGE—Christine Rimmer

Bravo Family Ties

Lovers turned best friends Matt Bravo and Corrine Lonnigan had been there, done that with each other, and had a beautiful daughter. But their affair was ancient history…until old flames reignited over the holidays—and Corrine made Matt a proud daddy yet again!

#2013 A COLD CREEK HOLIDAY—RaeAnne Thayne

The Cowboys of Cold Creek

Christmas had always made designer Emery Kendall sad. But this Cold Creek Christmas was different—she rediscovered her roots… and found the gift of true love with rancher Nate Cavazos, whose matchmaking nieces steered Emery and Nate to the mistletoe.

#2014 A NANNY UNDER THE MISTLETOE—
Teresa Southwick

The Nanny Network

Libby Bradford had nothing in common with playboy Jess Donnelly—except for their love of the very special little girl in Jess and Libby's care. But the more time Libby spent with her billionaire boss, the more the mistletoe beckoned.…

#2015 A WEAVER HOLIDAY HOMECOMING—Allison Leigh

Men of the Double-C Ranch

Former agent Ryan Clay just wanted to forget his past. Then Dr. Mallory Keegan came to town—with the child he never knew he had. Soon, Ryan discovered the joy only a Christmas spent with the little girl—and her beautiful Aunt Mallory—could bring.

#2016 THE TEXAS TYCOON'S CHRISTMAS BABY—
Brenda Harlen

The Foleys and the McCords

When Penny McCord found out her lover Jason Foley was using her to get info about her family's jewelry-store empire, she was doubly devastated—for Penny was pregnant. Would a Christmas miracle reunite them…and reconcile their feuding families for good?